NEWSPRINTS

For the young time travelers.
May the next era you land in be a little kinder than the last.

Library of Congress Control Number: 2016938202

ISBN 978-0-545-80311-3 (hardcover)
ISBN 978-0-545-80312-0 (paperback)

10 9 8 7 6 5 4 3 2 1   17 18 19 20 21
Printed in China   38
First edition, February 2017
Edited by Cassandra Pelham
Book design by Ru Xu and Phil Falco
Creative Director: David Saylor

NEWSPRINTS

Ru Xu

graphix
AN IMPRINT OF
SCHOLASTIC

The Sleepy Port City of Nautilene

PLASH
HUFF HUFF
♪
GOLDIE, THERE YOU ARE!
THEY STILL ON MY TAIL?
CATCH ME IF YOU CAN, YA TWEEDLE DUMS!
GET BACK HERE, BUGLE BRAT!

OOH!
BUILD SHIPS
WHAT D'YOU THINK?
CLIMB THE LADDER?
HEY!
GOOD CALL.
...
GOTCHA!
DONK
GAH!

CREAK
WHOA.
NEWS
WHOA!

HEY, HELLO?
ANYONE HERE?

Y'KNOW, GOLDIE...
I SEEM TO RECALL THE NAVY'S BUYING UP SCRAP METAL FOR **BIG BUCKS.**
IF THIS PLACE IS ABANDONED...
WE SHOULD DEFINITELY COME BACK.

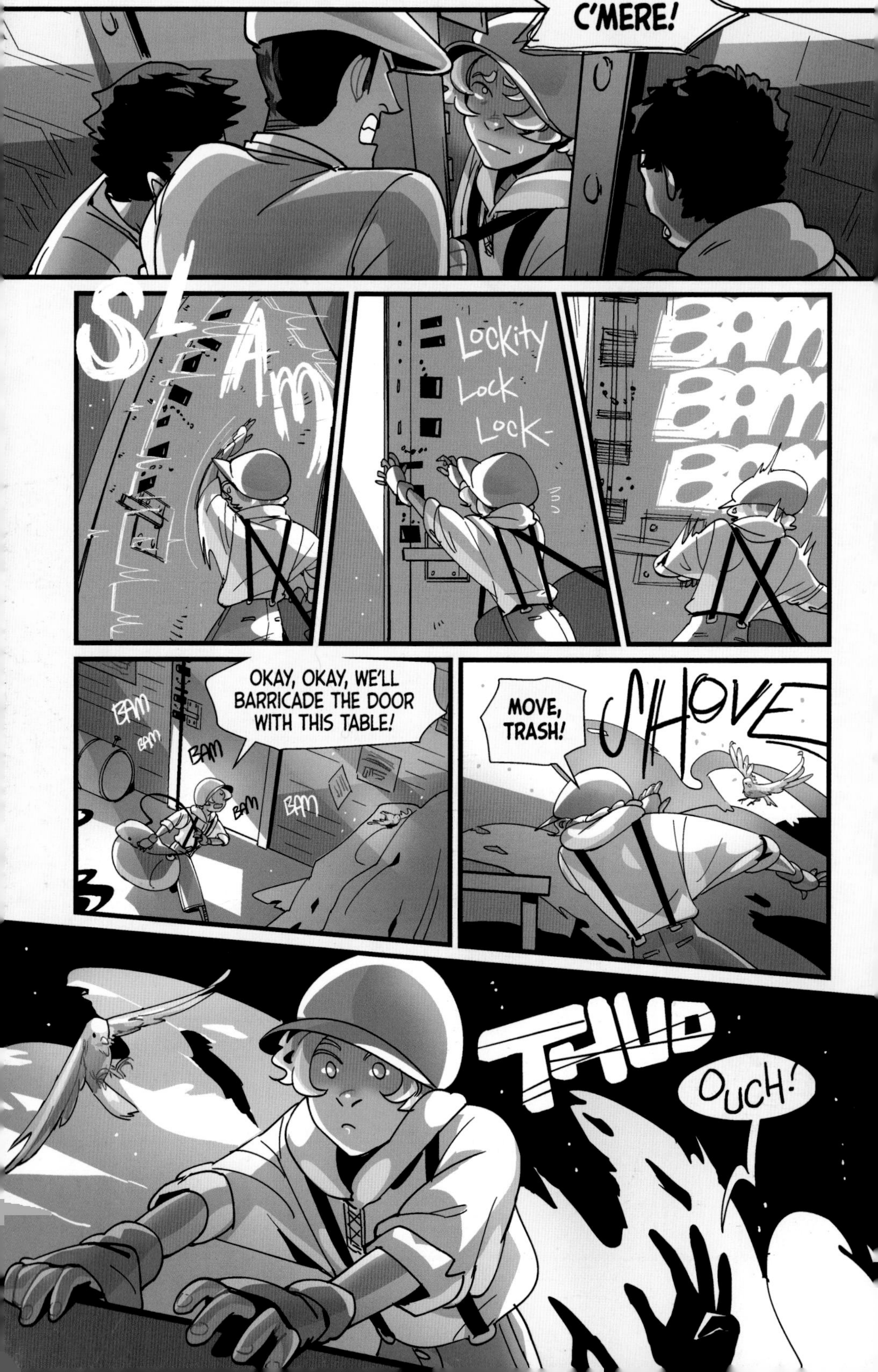
C'MERE!
SLAM
Lockity
Lock
Lock-
BAM
BAM
BAM
OKAY, OKAY, WE'LL BARRICADE THE DOOR WITH THIS TABLE!
BAM
BAM
BAM
BAM
BAM
MOVE, TRASH!
SHOVE
THUD
OUCH!

HUH?
GOOD GOOSE BUMPS!

YOUNG MAN.
YOU ARE NOT SUPPOSED TO BE...
Peck
Peck
Peck
OH, A CANARY!
I...I MEAN!
HOW DID YOU GET IN HERE?
BAM
BAM
BAM
THE DOOR WAS LOCKED!
IT SURE WAS.
YOU OUGHT TO PUT LOCKS ON YOUR WINDOWS FOR GOOD MEASURE!
heh
smack
SO, UHH, CAN I STAY TILL THEY LEAVE, OR WHAT?
BAM BAM BAM BAM BAM BAM BAM BAM BAM BAM BAM BAM BAM BAM

TWO HOURS LATER
CORRECT ME IF I'M WRONG, BUT THEY DON'T SEEM LIKE YOUR FRIENDS.
RIVAL NEWSIES. I WAS SELLING PAPERS ON THEIR TURF.
BAD GAMBLE. NOW I'M GONNA MISS CURFEW AND BE GROUNDED!
HMM, WHAT IF I WROTE YOUR GUARDIAN A NOTE OF EXCUSE?

LIKE: "THANKS, YOUR KID WOKE ME UP BEFORE I SUFFOCATED IN STEAM"?
BINGO!
GASP
I'LL JUST TEAR A PAGE OUT OF MY JOURNAL HERE...
IS THAT GOLD?
AWAH
WAIT, ISN'T THIS BOOK VALUABLE?
WELL, SURE! IT'S FULL OF MY MATH THEORIES!
MATH, HUH? LIKE COUNTING MONEY AND STUFF? YOU'RE SPEAKIN' MY LANGUAGE.
I LIKE TO THINK I WAS PRETTY GOOD AT THAT...
I MEAN, BACK WHEN I STILL WENT TO SCHOOL.
YOU AREN'T IN SCHOOL?
WHAT ABOUT YOUR EDUCATION?!

YOU KNOW HOW IT IS, WITH THE GRAND WAR AND ALL. EVERYONE'S DIRT POOR.
WE'RE DOWN TO SELLING OUR POTS AND PANS TO THE NAVY.
OH NO!
I'VE ALREADY GOT A JOB AT THE BUGLE, SO IT'S NOT LIKE I NEED TO GO TO SCHOOL.
MIGHT NOT LAST FOREVER, BUT...
A MIND THAT WANTS TO LEARN IS SUCH A SHAME TO WASTE!
WHAT IF I PAID YOU TO BE MY APPRENTICE?!
WHAT'S THE CATCH?
NOTHING! ALLOW ME TO WRITE A PLEA TO YOUR GUARDIAN!
DID YA HEAR THAT, GOLDIE?
THERE MIGHT BE EXTRA MILLET FOR YOU THIS WINTER!
BY THE WAY...

I DON'T HEAR ANY MORE OF THAT HORRID BANGING.
AHH, IT SEEMS THAT YOUR PURSUERS HAVE GIVEN UP!
OH GOOD, THERE'S STILL SOME DAY-LIGHT LEFT.
UMM, WAIT! NAMES!
I'M JACK!
I'LL DO MY BEST TO BE A GOOD TEACHER!

THANKS.
I'M BLUE.

Y REELECTION BY LANDSLIDE
E BUGLE OPENS DOORS
NAUTILENE'S ORPHAN BOYS
WE'RE THE BUGLE BOYS
The Nautilene Bugle
BUGLE NEWS
BUGLE'S RIVALRY WITH THE GRUNDIES MEAN TURF DISPUTE?
NAUTILENE ON STRICT RATIONS, BUT "I WILL PROTECT OUR PEACE!" SAYS MAYOR ARIC NANCY

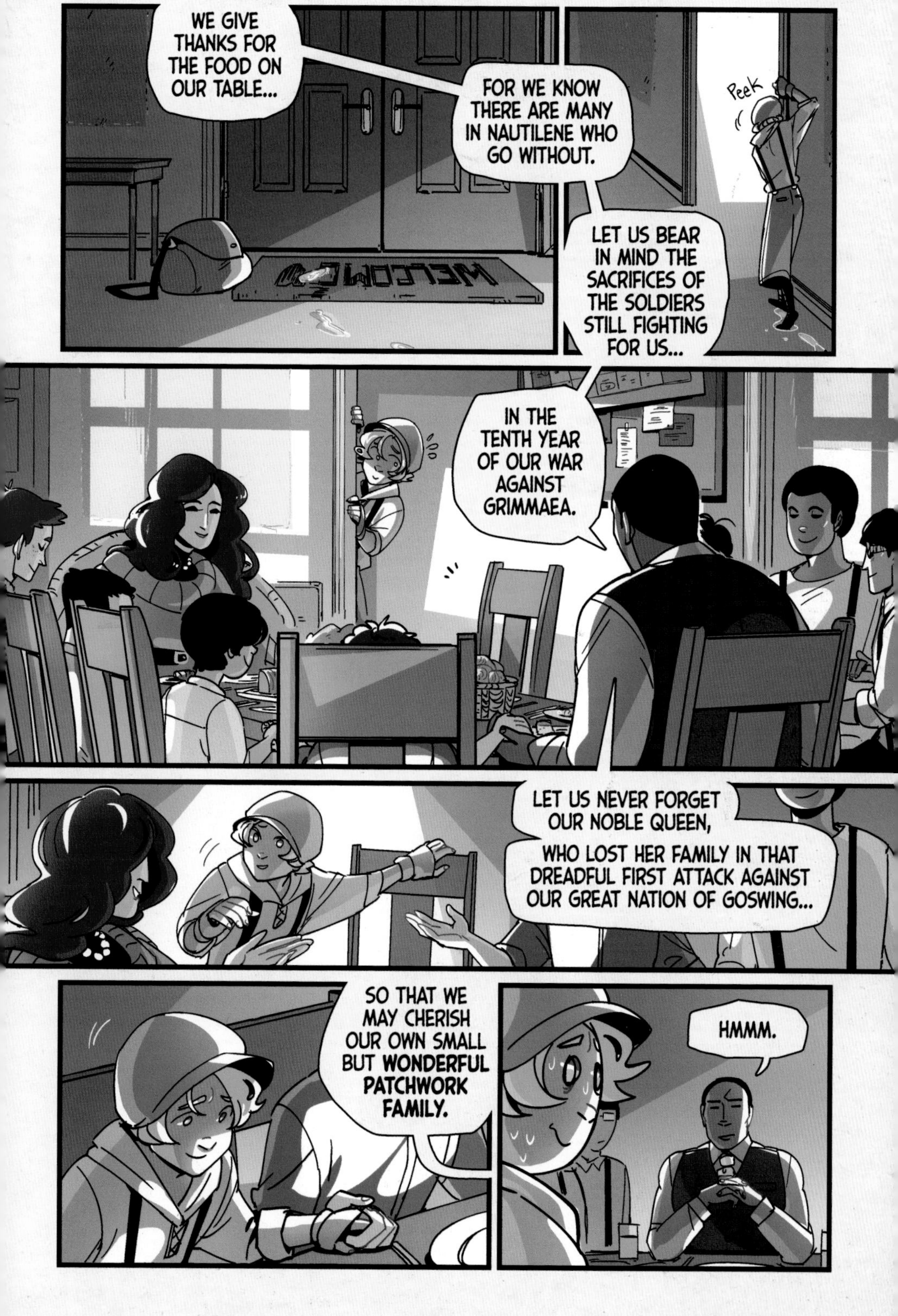
WE GIVE THANKS FOR THE FOOD ON OUR TABLE...
FOR WE KNOW THERE ARE MANY IN NAUTILENE WHO GO WITHOUT.
Peek
LET US BEAR IN MIND THE SACRIFICES OF THE SOLDIERS STILL FIGHTING FOR US...
IN THE TENTH YEAR OF OUR WAR AGAINST GRIMMAEA.
LET US NEVER FORGET OUR NOBLE QUEEN,
WHO LOST HER FAMILY IN THAT DREADFUL FIRST ATTACK AGAINST OUR GREAT NATION OF GOSWING...
SO THAT WE MAY CHERISH OUR OWN SMALL BUT **WONDERFUL PATCHWORK FAMILY.**
HMMM.

AHEM...
tap tap
WE ARE THANKFUL.
WE ARE THANKFUL!
NOW THEN, LET'S EAT!
SO, THE WAR STARTED 'CAUSE GRIMMAEA ATTACKED OUR ROYAL FAMILY, RIGHT?
munch munch
TODAY'S BUGLE SAID THAT IT STARTED BECAUSE OF A BORDER DISPUTE BETWEEN GOSWING AND GRIMMAEA.
BLUE, YOU READ THE BUGLE?
OF COURSE. EVERY DAY!

I WANNA KNOW WHAT'S GOING ON **OUTSIDE** THE CITY,
AND NO OTHER PAPER IN NAUTILENE TELLS THE **TRUTH!**
WELL, WE'VE ALWAYS BEEN PROUD OF THE **BUGLE'S INTEGRITY.**
OH, ARIC, DARLING! THAT REMINDS ME.
I'D LIKE TO LOOK OVER THE WORK BY YOUR NEW HIRES IN EDITORIAL.
I DON'T KNOW ABOUT **THAT,** MUFFY.
BETWEEN RUNNING THE HOUSE AND TAKING CARE OF THE BOYS,
I HARDLY THINK YOU HAVE TIME FOR THE BUSINESS.
UH.
YOU MAKE A POINT...
BUT MAYOR NANCY!
I THINK SHE'D BE GOOD AT THAT!
SHE'S BEEN TEACHING US ABOUT HOW JOURNALISTS WRITE THEIR ARTICLES!
YEAH, SHE USES EACH DAY'S NEWSPAPERS AS EXAMPLES.
I CAN WRITE AT A **SIXTH-GRADE** LEVEL NOW!
INDEED? HMM. WELL, IF THE BOYS THINK IT'S A GOOD IDEA, THEN I HAVE NO COMPLAINTS.

DARLING, I WON'T LET YOU DOWN!
HOW WONDERFUL!
WELL, THAT WAS AWKWARD.
IT'S LIKE HE DOESN'T REALLY WANT YOU TO HELP WITH THE FAMILY BUSINESS.
DON'T MIND ARIC. HE'S A LITTLE OLD-FASHIONED.
SPLASH
I'M LUCKY THERE'S A STRONG-WILLED GIRL HERE TO STAND UP FOR ME.

I APPRECIATE THAT YOU'VE KEPT MY SECRET FOR THREE YEARS.
OH, I'M SO GLAD TO HAVE YOU HERE!
I THINK YOUR NEW PAPER ROUTES HAVE REALLY HELPED US GET THE BUGLE OUT THERE!
MA'AM...
WHAT IS IT, BLUE?
DO YOU THINK I'VE... PROVEN MYSELF?
Y'THINK THEY'D STILL LET ME BE A NEWSBOY IF THEY KNEW I'M NOT A BOY?
DUCKLING, IF ANYONE'S PROOF THAT NEWSIES DON'T HAVE TO BE BOYS, IT'S YOU.

YEAH...I WANNA KEEP WORKING AT THE BUGLE.
WHEN THE TIME COMES, I WANNA BE THAT PERSON HANDING OUT NEWS WITH THE HEADLINE "WAR IS OVER!"
BUT I JUST DON'T KNOW...
I DON'T WANNA TAKE THE CHANCE THAT THE GUYS WON'T SEE ME THE SAME WAY ANYMORE.
BUT WE'RE ALL GROWING UP, AND THEY'RE GOING TO NOTICE OUR DIFFERENCES SOONER OR LATER...
I SHOULD TELL THEM, RIGHT?
IT'S UP TO YOU!
IF THEY DON'T LIKE IT, THERE'S ALWAYS A PLACE FOR YOU IN OUR AFFILIATE GIRLS' HOME.
fuu
BUT I DON'T WANT ANYTHING TO CHANGE...
OH! LET ME TELL YOU ABOUT WHAT HAPPENED TO ME TODAY.
THE GRUNDIES CHASED ME TO THAT WEIRD BUILDING WITH THE CURVED ROOF...

JACK, I'M HERE!
BLUE! GOOD TIMING!
HELP ME PUT OUT THE SMALL FIRES!
OW! NOW I'M ON FIRE!
Day One as Jack's Apprentice

Day Two
I'M SO SORRY, MY MIND IS ON A MILLION OTHER THINGS RIGHT NOW.
Day Three
NOW THESE FREQUENCIES WILL ATTRACT CERTAIN TYPES OF BIRDS...
BUT I CAN'T REMEMBER THE RIGHT NUMBER FOR THE MACHINE.
RAVENS GULLS SANDERLINGS
WHAT FREQUENCY DID THOSE DARNED CORVIDS LIKE...?
THREE FOUR EIGHT..? THOUSAND?
I HAVEN'T A CLUE WHAT YOU'RE...
DID I LOCK THE FRONT DOOR?
HUH?
Day Four
OBSERVE, BLUE! THE BIRDS ARE ATTRACTED TO THIS FREQUENCY!
YOU KNOW GULLS WILL CHASE YOU FOR CHOPPED LIVER, RIGHT?

Day Five

Day Six

Day Seven

UGH
WE'RE ON THE FRONT PAGE OF EVERY NEWSPAPER IN NAUTILENE!
CAN YOU GET THE ADDRESS OF THAT PAWN SHOP FOR ME?

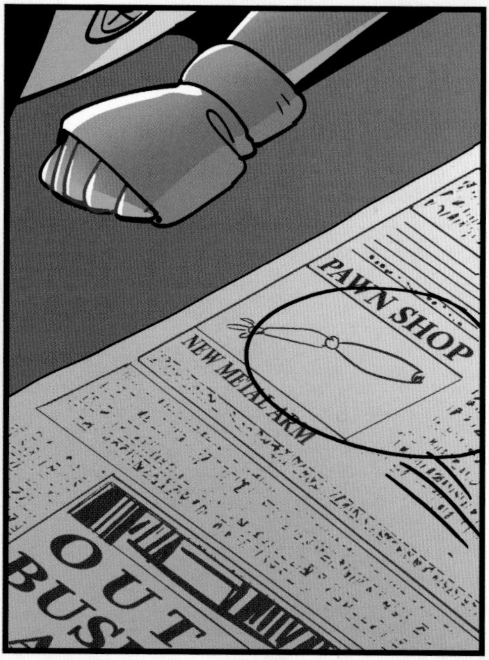
PAWN SHOP
NEW METAL ARM

OPEN
PAWN

RING-A-LING
THIS IS PRETTY!
YOU PUT DOWN THAT DOLL RIGHT NOW.
IT'S NOT FOR YOU, YOUNG MAN.
OH, I'LL BE CAREFUL! I WAS JUST LOOKING!

I'D LIKE IT TO GO TO THE HOME OF A NICE GIRL.
CAN'T DO THAT IF IT'S BROKEN, HMM?
...
UMM, ABOUT THIS METAL ARM...WHERE DID YOU FIND IT?
DON'T KNOW, DEAR. THE DOG FOUND IT.
A DOG, HUH?
YOU'RE FLUFFY!
thmp
thmp
HUH
GAH!

JACK! HELP
BLUE!
BAD DOG!
BOW WOW

JACK, IT'S GONNA EAT ME! HELP!
I'LL BUY THIS ARM RIGHT NOW.
A FINE IDEA. ALL UNSOLD METAL GOES TO THE NAVY AT THE END OF THE WEEK.
JACK!
KA-TING!
YUCK!
WHAT A PRODUCTIVE DAY!
IF YA SAY SO...
glance
OH, GOOSE BUTTS!

WHAT'S WRONG, BLUE?
OUT OF BUSINESS
HIDE ME!
OH.
IT'S THOSE BOYS WHO WERE CHASING YOU.
JACK, LET'S GO!
IF THEY SEE ME HERE, THEY'LL BEAT UP ME AND MY FRIENDS!
THAT'S VERY... MEAN.
OUT OF BUSINESS
SHOP
MAYBE I CAN HELP.

bzz
bzzzz
bzzzzzz
bzzz
Z Z Z Z Z Z

NAUTILENE NAVAL BASE
OUR GIRLS BUILDING SHIPS OUR BOYS ARE SAILING TO WAR!
NAUTILENE - Away from the battlefield, a minor repair station for the navy.
WOMEN OF GOSWING
UILD SHIPS
HERO ADMIRAL OVERSE
NAUTILENE NAVAL B

HERE, BLUE.
I MADE THIS FOR YOU.
The Nautilene Naval Base
A PIN!
HA, THAT'S PRETTY CUTE. IT'S GOLDIE!
THIS STUFF INSIDE...AHA!
WE PULLED IT OUTTA THAT WEIRD METAL ARM.
WOW!

WELL, I THOUGHT IT'D BE MORE USEFUL TO **YOU** THAN AT MY PLACE.
YOU SEE, BLUE, THIS PIN IS A **TRACKING DEVICE.**
WHAT'S THAT?
IF YOU PRESS THE BUTTON, IT'LL ACTIVATE A **SEEKING DEVICE** THAT WILL LOCATE IT.
IT'S NOT QUITE READY FOR CIVILIAN USE...
SO IT'S ONLY FOR **EMERGENCIES!**
THAT... ACTUALLY SOUNDS REALLY USEFUL.
AND HERE I THOUGHT YOU WERE ONLY GOOD AT BREAKING RADIOS!
NONSENSE. I'M A MAN OF MANY TALENTS.

AND THAT'S EVERYTHING?
I'LL RELAY YOUR CONCERNS ABOUT THE WORKING CONDITIONS TO THE ADMIRAL...
OH!
NO, STOP RIGHT THERE.
ME?
SIR, YOU MAY NOT BRING YOUR SON HERE.
I'M AN **APPRENTICE,** MA'AM!
CHILDREN AREN'T ALLOWED AT THE NAVAL BASE.
MISS, SURELY HE WON'T BE A PROBLEM?
COULD I TALK TO A SUPERIOR OFFICER, OR...
ADULTS GET LOST FOR DAYS IN THIS GIANT BASE, AND CHILDREN MORE SO.
PLEASE ESCORT YOUR CHILD OUT.
WOW.

LET'S LISTEN TO THE LADY.
I'LL JUST TAKE A TAXI BACK.
YOU'RE LEAVING ME HERE?
UM, OKAY. WOW... M-MY APOLOGIES.
SEE, I MADE AN APPOINTMENT BY POST TO SEE THE ADMIRAL TODAY.
NOON APPOINTMENT? YOU MUST BE JACK. PLEASE FOLLOW ME.
GOLDIE, COME BACK!
YOU DIDN'T INCLUDE YOUR FULL NAME.
I DON'T LIKE TO GO BY IT.
HMM... UNUSUAL.

IT'S ALSO UNUSUAL TO SEE THE EMPLOYMENT OF A MIXED CHILD.
WHO? BLUE?
HE HAS PALE EYES LIKE US, BUT THAT SHOCK OF LIGHT HAIR IS DEFINITELY GRIMMAEAN.
I'M HAPPY, IS WHAT I'M SAYING.
THESE DAYS, PEOPLE FROM THE CAPITAL USUALLY DON'T TAKE WELL TO ANYONE WITH GRIMMAEAN BLOOD.
HOW'D YOU KNOW THAT I'M FROM ALTALUS?
YOU'RE NOT THE FIRST BLACK UNIFORM I'VE SEEN.
MY FATHER AND I USED TO LIVE IN THE CAPITAL.
REALLY? WHICH DISTRICT?

WOW, THAT LADY WASN'T KIDDING ABOUT GETTING LOST.
HOW'D WE GET ALL THE WAY UP HERE?
THOUGH, THIS PLACE ISN'T HALF BAD, HUH?
EVEN WITH ALL THESE CROWS, IT'S PRETTY SWANKY!

AND IF THERE ARE TOUGH LADIES MANAGING NAVAL BASES...
MAYBE I COULD WORK HERE WHEN I GROW UP.
AH

H-HEY! IT'S DANGEROUS UP THERE!
AAAAAAAUGH
THE BIRDS ARE FINE
YEAH, THAT'S 'CAUSE THEY CAN FLY!
I CAN FLY TOO
JUST NOT RIGHT NOW
slip
OH.
OH!
GOOSE BUTTS!

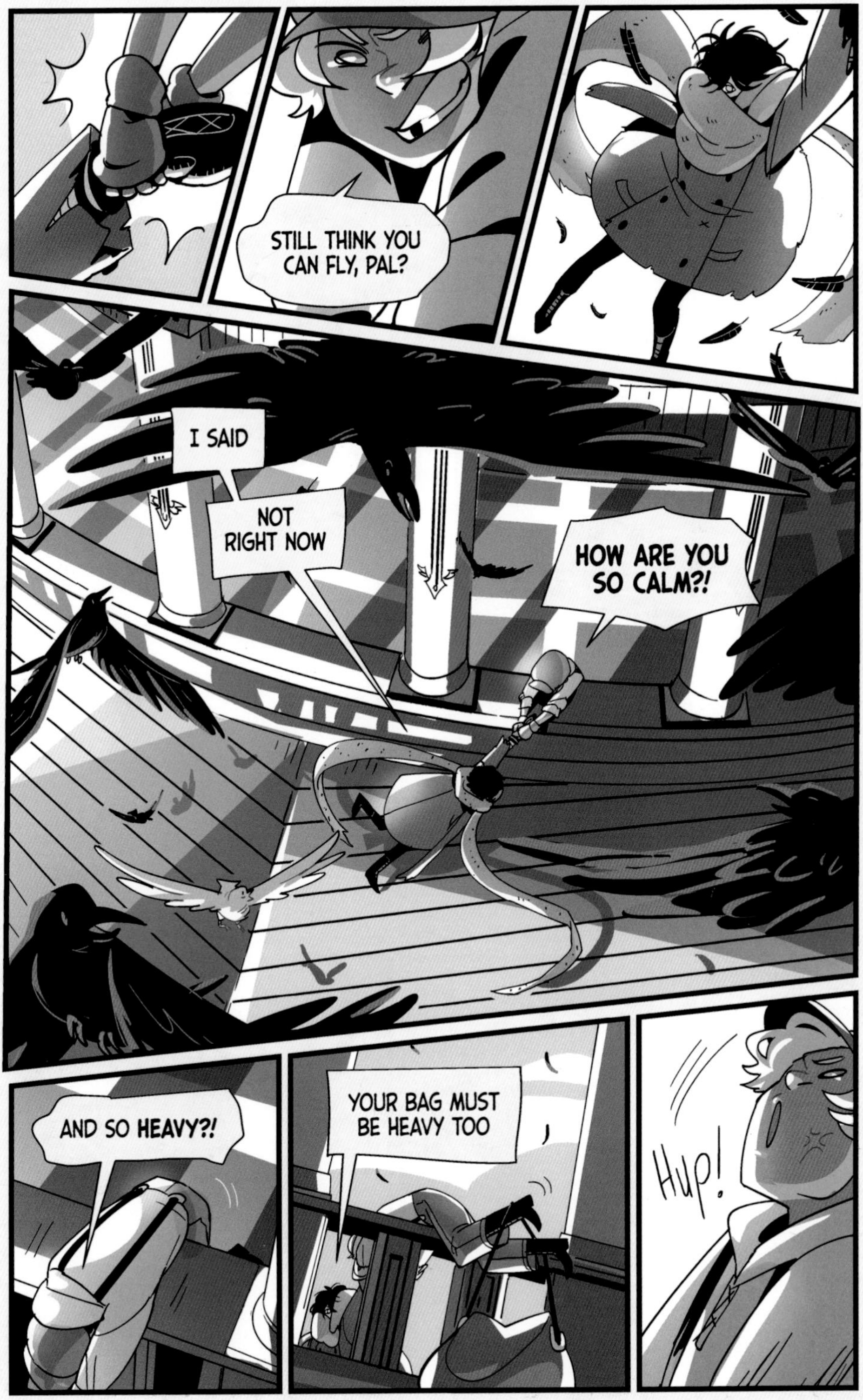
STILL THINK YOU CAN FLY, PAL?
I SAID
NOT RIGHT NOW
HOW ARE YOU SO CALM?!
AND SO HEAVY?!
YOUR BAG MUST BE HEAVY TOO
Hup!

WHEW!
LISTEN HERE, HUMPTY DUMPTY, YOU STAY OFF THE ROOF!
NO
NO?! WHAT IF YA FALL AGAIN?!
MAYBE YOU WILL CATCH ME AGAIN

Y'KNOW, I'M KINDA FEELIN' LIKE...
MAYBE I OUGHT TO THROW YOUR UNGRATEFUL BUTT OFF THE ROOF **MYSELF!**
PLEASE DON'T
IT'S PEACEFUL UP THERE
WHEN IT'S JUST THE BIRDS AND ME
THEY LIKE THE SOUNDS MY HEAD MAKES
I DIDN'T LIKE THE CITY SO I CAME HERE
WELL, IT LOOKS LIKE THE BIRDS FOLLOWED YOU.
GOLDIE SEEMS TO LIKE YOU ALL RIGHT.
FIIIINE, IF YOU'RE NICE TO GOLDIE...
THEN I GUESS I DON'T MIND SAVING YOU EVERY ONCE IN A WHILE.

NAME'S BLUE.
I'M A NEWSIE.
WHAT ABOUT YOU?
I AM
I AM CROW
JUST **CROW**, HUH?
YOU AND YOUR FAMILY LIVE AROUND HERE?
I DON'T HAVE FAMILY

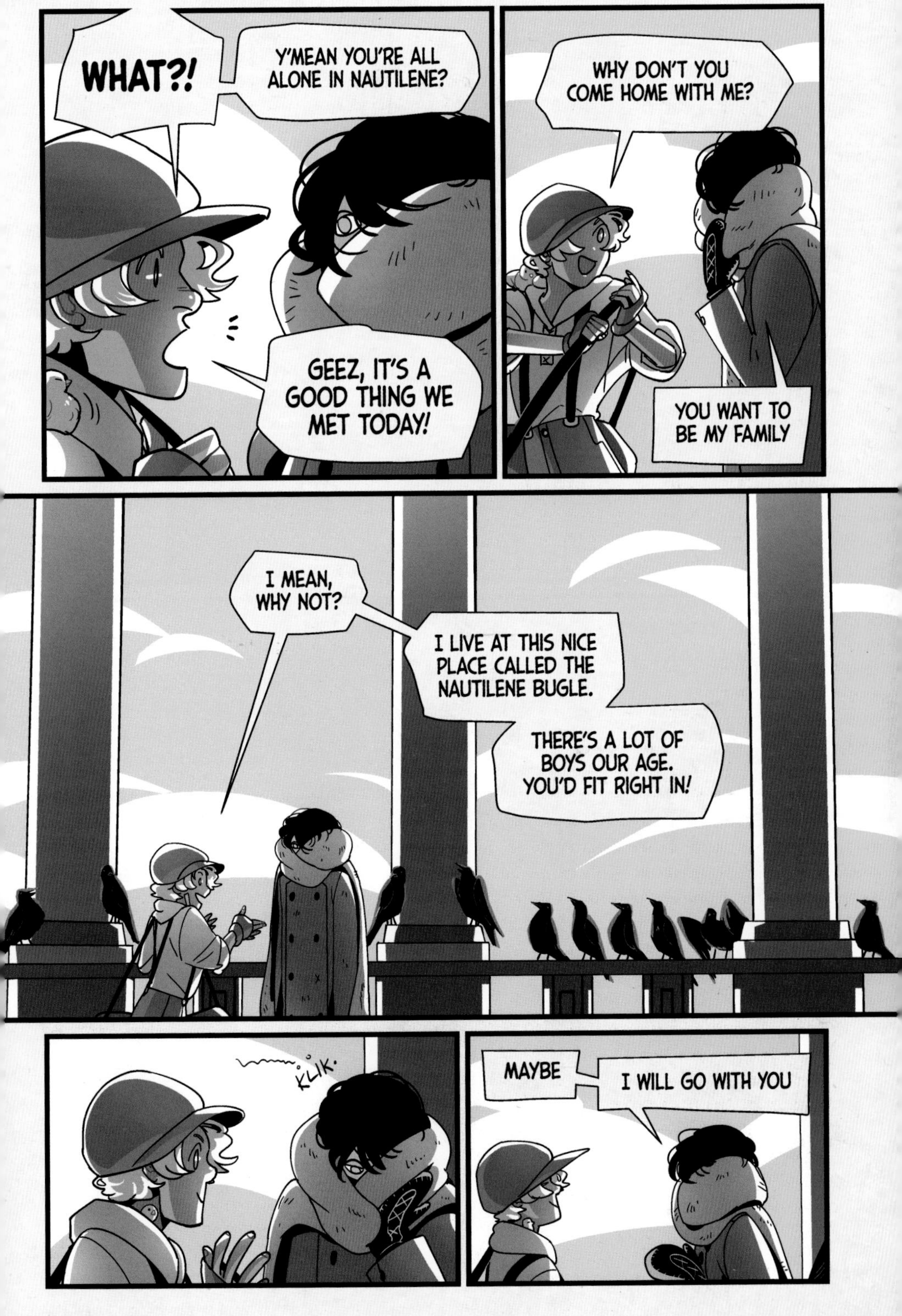
WHAT?!
Y'MEAN YOU'RE ALL ALONE IN NAUTILENE?
GEEZ, IT'S A GOOD THING WE MET TODAY!
WHY DON'T YOU COME HOME WITH ME?
YOU WANT TO BE MY FAMILY
I MEAN, WHY NOT?
I LIVE AT THIS NICE PLACE CALLED THE NAUTILENE BUGLE.
THERE'S A LOT OF BOYS OUR AGE. YOU'D FIT RIGHT IN!
KLIK.
MAYBE
I WILL GO WITH YOU

GREAT!
BUT FIRST LET'S GET OUTTA HERE FAST!
GRAB
RIGHT NOW
DEFINITELY!
I DUNNO HOW YOU GOT IN, BUT...
THE GROWN-UPS GET PRETTY ANGRY WHEN THEY FIND KIDS HERE.
TRUE
SIR, IF YOU'D JUST PLEASE RESPOND--
BLUE
SO I--
BUMP
ADMIRAL, SIR, LOOK OUT!
ANGRY GROWN-UP
ADMIRAL...?
UH-OH.

HOLD THAT THOUGHT, OFFICER.
UHH, SIR.
VERY ANGRY
WHY ARE THERE ERRANT CHILDREN RUNNING AROUND MY NAVAL BASE?
GO GET THAT BOY!
WAIT! HOLD ON!
WELL? DO THEY TRAIN YOU TO STAND THERE USELESSLY?
N-NO, OF COURSE NOT, SIR.
PAT PAT
GOLDIE?
BUT I'M JUST A SECRETARY, ADMIRAL REED!
CROW, DON'T CLIMB THAT!

GO ON.
COME BACK...
UM, SIR. I'M SORRY. WE WERE JUST LEAVING. SIR.
LITTLE BOY, YOU DO NOT COME HERE TO PLAY SAILOR. DO YOU UNDERSTAND?
FOLLOW ME.
YES...SIR.
KLOK

KLOK
KLOK
KLOK
KLOK
YOU ARE LOOKING FOR...?
A COMPLEX MACHINE.
WE HAVE PLENTY OF THOSE.
YOU'LL HAVE TO BE MORE SPECIFIC!
SO THEN, YOU HAVEN'T SEEN ANYTHING OUT OF THE ORDINARY--
JILL, REPORT.
WHOA!
UH, SIR!

FINISHED MY WORK, FATHER. YOU HAVE MEETINGS SCHEDULED ALL MORNING AND AFTERNOON.
IN
OUT
THAT'S MY GIRL. HAVE THE REST OF THE DAY OFF.
AND TAKE THIS BOY HOME.
MAKE SURE HIS GUARDIANS GIVE HIM A STERN TALKING TO.
HMM? WHO'S THIS?
YOUR NOON APPOINT-MENT.
JACK.
ANOTHER BLACK UNIFORM?
WHY ARE THERE SO MANY ALTALUS OFFICIALS AROUND?
NO, NO! I'M RETIRED. PLEASE DON'T TELL THEM I'M HERE, SIR!
ALTALUS.
I GUESS THAT MAKES SENSE.
I'VE NEVER SEEN THAT UNIFORM IN NAUTILENE BEFORE.

THERE'S NOTHING TO REPORT.
TELL THE QUEEN THAT NAUTILENE IS AS DULL AS ALWAYS.
I'M NOT HERE ON BEHALF OF THE QUEEN, SIR.
IN FACT, I'D HOPED TO REACH OUT TO YOU BEFORE THE OTHERS DID.
SIR, I BELIEVE THERE IS A DANGEROUS WEAPON IN YOUR CITY.
ALL I CAN TELL YOU IS THAT IT IS DRAWN TO OTHER MACHINES.
...I SEE.
AND YOU SAY THE CAPITAL IS NOT INVOLVED?
WHO ARE YOU, JACK?
I'M A CONCERNED CITIZEN, SIR.

hmm
um
IT SEEMS TO ME LIKE YOU KINDA RUN THIS PLACE.
THE ADMIRAL IS MY FATHER.
HIS SECRETARY WAS DRAFTED, SO I FILL IN WHERE I CAN.
ARE THERE MORE LADIES LIKE YOU HERE?
WELL, THOSE WOMEN I WAS TALKING TO EARLIER BUILD AND REPAIR THE SHIPS OUTSIDE.
OH! I THINK THEY WERE FEATURED IN THE BUGLE A COUPLE YEARS AGO!
PAT PAT

I READ THEY HAVE TO STEP DOWN WHEN THE MEN COME BACK FROM THE WAR.
BUT THEY'RE DOING A FINE JOB NOW, AREN'T THEY?
IT'S SAID THESE SHIPS CAN SURVIVE MORE BATTLES THAN ANY OF THE GRIMMAEANS' SHIPS!
IF THE ADMIRAL'S ORIGINAL SECRETARY COMES BACK, D'YOU HAVE TO GIVE UP YOUR JOB, TOO?
IF HE WANTS IT, I SUPPOSE I WILL. HE'LL BE A VETERAN.
AND THEN WHAT WOULD YOU DO?
HMM. MAYBE I'LL HAVE TO FIND A JOB MORE "SUITABLE" FOR A LADY.
OR MAYBE I'LL FINALLY GET MARRIED LIKE MY FATHER WANTS,
AND THEN STAY HOME TO RAISE SOME CUTE RASCALS LIKE YOU.
GAH!
HERE'S AN IDEA FOR YA!
IF YOU MARRY A MAN WHO'D RATHER BE AT HOME, YOU CAN KEEP WORKING.
Y'KNOW, A GUY LIKE JACK!
OH? YOU THINK SO?

AND SINCE THE ADMIRAL'S YOUR POPS, **SURELY** YOU COULD GET ANOTHER JOB HERE!
AND OKAY, PEOPLE MIGHT POINT AND WHISPER, BUT THE MOST IMPORTANT THING IS THAT...
YOU CAN **CHOOSE** WHAT TO DO WITH YOUR OWN LIFE!
IF YOU HAVE A PLACE YOU **BELONG,** WHY SHOULDN'T YOU TRY TO **KEEP** IT?
WHO CARES IF TOTAL STRANGERS THINK NEWSIES CAN ONLY BE BOYS?!
OH, HAVE I FORGOTTEN TO TELL YA THAT I'M A NEWSBOY, HAHA?
SO YOU **ARE...**

I KNOW I SAID THAT CHILDREN AREN'T ALLOWED AT THE BASE,
BUT IF YOU STAY WITH ME, I CAN SHOW YOU AROUND.
PERHAPS INTRODUCE YOU TO SOME OF THE SHIPBUILDERS HERE.
WOULD YOU, MA'AM?!
CALL ME JILL.
JILL. MY NAME IS...
BLUE.
IT'S NICE TO MEET YOU, BLUE.
DO YOU HAVE ANY QUESTIONS FOR ME ABOUT WORKING HERE?
DO I EVER.

SO, IF YOU HAVE TIME, YOU SHOULD DEFINITELY VISIT JACK AND ME AT HIS STUDIO.
I'D LIKE THAT!
KLIK
CROW!
GOLDIE!
GROWN-UP
DON'T WORRY, JILL'S ALL RIGHT. SHE'LL TAKE US BACK TO NAUTILENE!
NO GROWN-UPS
NO CITIES
JILL'S GONNA DRIVE ME HOME.
HI!
AND I WANT YOU TO COME WITH US!

LOOK, SHE THINKS YOU'RE SWELL.
GROWN-UPS DON'T LIKE ME
I TRUST HER. WILL YOU TRUST ME?
KLIK
BLUE, WHY ARE THESE BIRDS FOLLOWING US?

BUGLE NEWS
HERE'S THE BUGLE! C'MON, I'LL INTRODUCE YOU TO EVERYONE!
I DON'T WANT TO GO INSIDE
THE GROWN-UPS WON'T LIKE ME
THEY WILL, TOO.
THE MAYOR AND MS. MUFFY ARE GOOD PEOPLE.
SO MAYBE YOU'RE A LITTLE WEIRD, BUT WHO ISN'T?

I MEAN, WAIT UNTIL YOU MEET JACK--
CROW?
CROW!
BUGLE NEWS

PAT'S

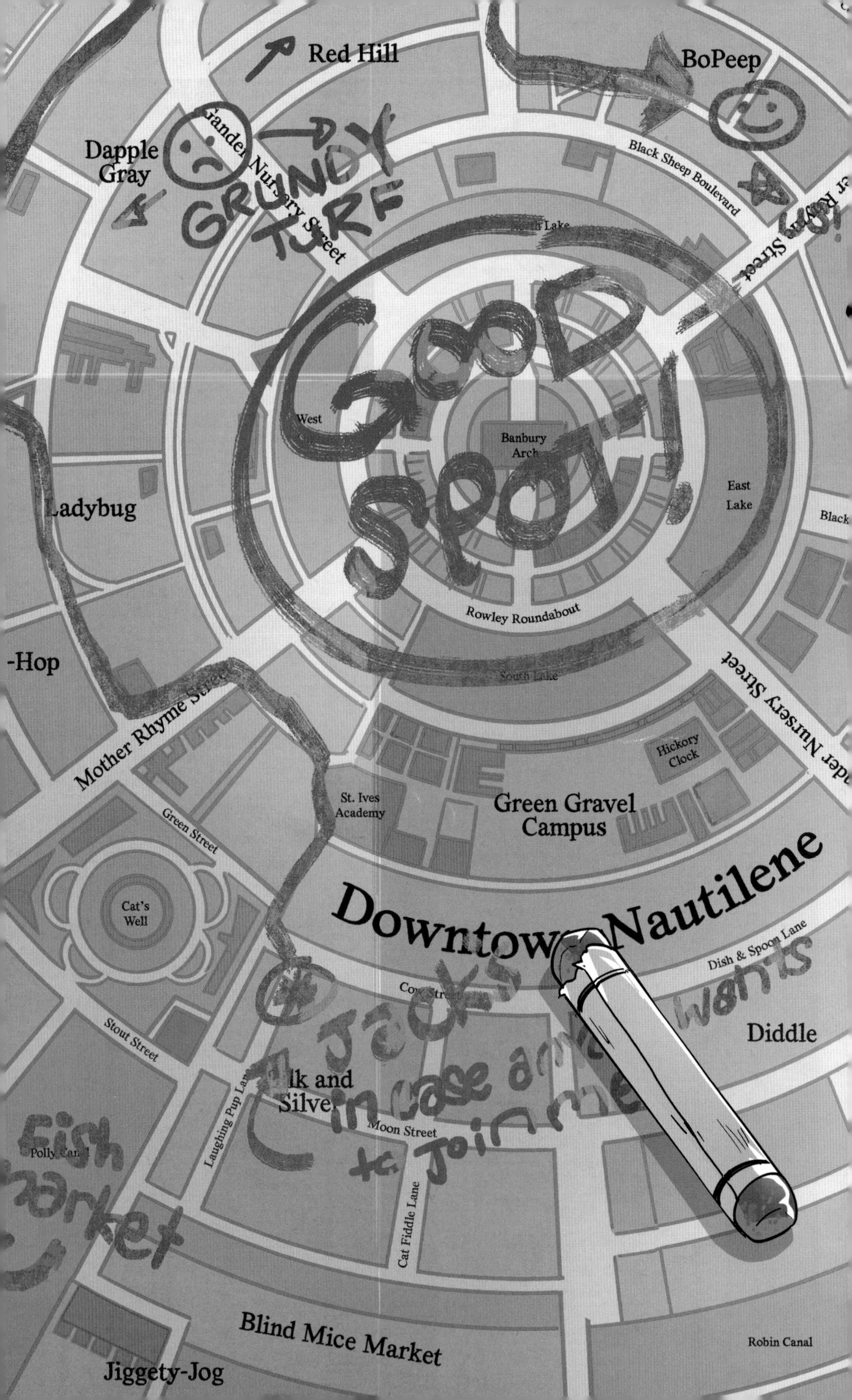
Red Hill
BoPeep
Dapple Gray
Gander Nursery Street
GRUNDY TURF
Black Sheep Boulevard
GOOD SPOT!
West
Banbury Arch
East Lake
Black
Ladybug
Rowley Roundabout
-Hop
South Lake
Mother Rhyme Street
Nursery Street
Hickory Clock
St. Ives Academy
Green Gravel Campus
Green Street
Cat's Well
Downtown Nautilene
Dish & Spoon Lane
Cow Street
Jack's
wants
Diddle
Stout Street
Laughing Pup Lane
lk and Silve
in case
to join me
Moon Street
Fish market
Cat Fiddle Lane
Blind Mice Market
Robin Canal
Jiggety-Jog

BUGLE NEWS
CATCH YOU GUYS LATER!
I'M HERE!
HEY, BLUE!
HELP ME PUT THESE AWAY.

SO I GET TO CHOOSE OUR NEXT PROJECT?
INDEED!
TA DA
HOW 'BOUT WE FINISH **THAT?**
IT'S A BIRD, RIGHT? LET'S GET IT TO FLY!
WELL, THAT'LL BE A DIFFICULT PROJECT.
FLIGHT IS **HARDLY** EVEN READY FOR MILITARY USE AS IT IS. IT'S DEFINITELY NOT READY FOR **CIVILIANS!**
BUT NEITHER WAS THIS GOLDIE PIN YOU MADE ME.
TRUE ENOUGH. I SUPPOSE THAT AS LONG AS WE TAKE SAFETY PRECAUTIONS...
BANG BANG
YEAH, **SAFELY** PUT A SEAT HERE, SO I CAN RIDE IN IT!
HARNESSING FLIGHT TO TRANSPORT CIVILIANS?!
MY, THAT'S... **THAT'S...**
THAT'S FOR THE **GREATER GOOD!** NOW YOU'VE CONVINCED ME!
BLUE, CAN YOU GRAB THOSE BLUEPRINTS?
YES, SIR!

BLUE.
I HOPE THIS AWFUL WAR ENDS BEFORE YOU AND YOUR FRIENDS REACH DRAFT AGE.
EHH, MOST OF THE BOYS AT THE BUGLE WON'T BE TWENTY-ONE FOR A WHILE.
EXCEPT HECTOR. HE'S THE ONE WHO BROUGHT ME TO THE BUGLE AFTER MY DAD...
...
SIGH
ANYHOOS.
SHFF
HECTOR'S IN ALTALUS NOW. HE'S A JOURNALIST. MAYBE YOU'VE READ SOME OF HIS STUFF!
I DIDN'T REALLY READ NEWSPAPERS UNTIL I MET YOU--
KNOK
KNOK
KNOK
I'LL GET THE DOOR!
HM?

BLUE!
HUNGRY?
JILL!
'SUP.
GUYS!
LET ME GUESS. YOU TWO JUST **HAPPENED** TO BE IN THE NEIGHBORHOOD?
YOU'RE SO KIND TO BRING LUNCH AGAIN! BUT YOU NEEDN'T IF IT'S TOO MUCH TROUBLE.
floof
I REALIZE IT'S A LONG DRIVE FROM THE BASE--
I'M JUST HAPPY TO MAKE SURE BLUE HAS A NICE LUNCH.
AND YOU SHOULD EAT, TOO.

WE'LL HELP YOU SELL THE REST OF YOUR PAPERS!
OH, JACK. I SAW MORE OF YOUR FELLOW BLACK UNIFORM OFFICERS TODAY.
ERM...
WELL, I PROBABLY DON'T KNOW ANY OF THEM. I'M RETIRED, REMEMBER?
HA HA
OH YEAH, BLUE. YOU OUGHTA KNOW, HECTOR'S VISITING!
WHEN?!
BYE, BLUE.
I HAVEN'T HEARD FROM HIM SINCE HE BOARDED THE TRAIN FOR ALTALUS.
I WAS GETTING WORRIED HE FORGOT ABOUT US.

EXTRA!
NAUTILENE BUGLE!
OH!
CROW!
I SHOULD'VE KNOWN GOLDIE WAS WITH YOU!
GUYS, THIS IS THE KID FROM THE NAVAL BASE!
CROW.

KAW
AWK
AWK
KAW
AWK
AWK
KAW
AWK
WOW
DO THAT AGAIN!
OKAY, STOP SHOWING OFF.
WE GOTTA WORK!
WOMEN OF GOSWING

huh?
AH!
WHEW!
WE GOT DONE EARLY TODAY!

HUH, MAYBE NOT BY MUCH.
LET'S GO HOME.
CROW, COME WITH US BACK TO THE BUGLE.
KLIK
HEY, WHAT'S WRONG?
DIDN'T YOU NOTICE THE GUYS LIKED YOU?
EVERYONE ELSE WILL LIKE YOU, TOO!
GROWN UPS DON'T LIKE ME
WHAT'S THAT MEAN?
I MEAN, SERIOUSLY, GIVE 'EM A CHANCE...

BUILD SHIPS
IN NAUTILENE
YOUR

YO
COU
WIN
JOHN AND PETER, GO DOWN-TOWN WITH THE BROTHERS.
GRUNDIES ARE GETTING EXTRA MEAN THIS WINTER, SO WATCH OUT FOR THEM.
YOU OKAY, BLUE?
YAWN
I'M FINE.

SEE YOU GUYS AT SUPPER!
SIGH
BUGLE!
ALTALUSIAN OFFICIALS ALL OVER NAUTILENE!
WHY ARE THEY HERE?
YAWN
EXTRA, EXTRA! READ ALL ABOUT IT IN THE BUGLE!
ALTALUSIAN OFFICIALS ALL OVER...
WHY ARE THEY...
HERE?
SWAY
shake shake
ONE FOR ME, DEAR.
READ ABOUT IT...

BUGLE.
YAWN
THUD
BLUE.
ZZZ

THIS IS NOT A PLACE YOU CAN SLEEP.
BLUE.

BUGLE NEWS
KNOK
KNOK
HEY.
!

fluff
NICE HAT.
HELLO TO YOU TOO, GOLDIE.
SO KIDDO, ARE YOU A NEW RECRUIT?
I THINK EVERYONE ELSE IS STILL OUT ON THEIR ROUTES.
HOW'D YOU END UP WITH BLUE'S HAT?
Y'KNOW, I GAVE THIS TO HIM.
I'M HECTOR, BY THE WAY.

Z
ZZZZZ
THIS IS BLUE'S HOME. BLUE SLEEPS HERE.
HAHA, THIS KID'S GIVEN YOU A LOTTA TROUBLE, HUH?
COME IN.
YOU CAN HANG OUT TILL BLUE WAKES UP.

IMPERIAL GOSWING

Inventor
Jack Dingle?
Note to self
suspicious

BUT WHERE IS THE BOY WHO LOOKS AFTER THE SHEEP?
BUT WHERE IS THE BOY WHO LOOKS AFTER THE SHEEP?
UNDER A HAYSTACK, FAST ASLEEP.
UNDER A HAYSTACK, FAST ASLEEP.
DANG, THAT'S PERFECT.
DANG, THAT'S PERFECT.
I GOT IT, KID. YOU CAN STOP COPYING ME NOW.
OH HEY, BLUE'S UP.

BLUE, DID YOU KNOW YOUR FRIEND IS GREAT AT MIMICRY?
CROW! PETER PICKED A PECK OF PICKLED PEPPERS!
PETER PICKED A PECK OF PICKLED PEPPERS!
PERFECT!
YEAH, I KNOW HE CAN DO THAT.
YOU SHOULD HEAR HIS BIRD CALLS.
BUT WHEN'D YOU GET BACK?!
A-AND HOW THE HECK'D YOU GET CROW TO COME INTO THE BUGLE?!
WAIT, WHAT AM I DOING HERE?
WHAT ABOUT MY ROUTE?
HOW LONG HAVE I BEEN OUT?
AN ENTIRE DAY?!

I LET EVERYONE DOWN...
NAH, THEY ALL WANTED TO PITCH IN WHILE YOU WERE ASLEEP.
YOUR CROW FRIEND KIND OF HOVERED OVER YOU THE ENTIRE TIME.
BUT IT'S NOT JUST THE BUGLE BEAT.
I'M WORRIED ABOUT MY PART-TIME JOB...
RIGHT, THE BOYS SAY YOU'RE THE ONE TO ASK ABOUT THAT...
'BOUT WHAT?
tap
tap
SERIOUSLY, YOU'VE BEEN KINDA FIDGETY SINCE YOU GOT BACK...
IT'S MAKIN' ME NERVOUS.

RIGHT, LET'S JUST SAY I WASN'T ONLY IN ALTALUS...
BUT, UHH... LIFE OF A WAR JOURNALIST.
NOW LISTEN, I'M WORKING ON THE BIGGEST STORY OF THE WAR, OKAY?
AND I THINK YOU CAN HELP ME.
ONE OF THE QUEEN'S ADVISORS IS MISSING.
THE SEARCH HAS GONE ON FOR MONTHS.
?
EVERYONE IN ALTALUS SAYS HE'S THE KEY TO WINNING THE WAR.
AND? YOU CAN BARELY SEE THE GUY IN THE PHOTO, HEC.
HE GOES BY JACK.
BUT DON'T YOU RECOGNIZE HIM?

THIS MAN'S A WILD CARD IN THE WAR.
I WANNA KNOW EVERY-THING ABOUT HIM...
BEFORE THE QUEEN'S MEN GET THEIR HANDS ON HIM AND DRAG HIM BACK TO ALTALUS.
A WILD CARD? MY BOSS ISN'T NEARLY THAT COOL.
shf shf
HE'S A BLACK UNIFORM OFFICIAL.
I BET HE'S INVOLVED WITH WEAPON DESIGN. A REAL GENIUS OF AN INVENTOR.
BLACK UNIFORM
INVENTOR
?
GENIUS
NAH, NOTHING MY BOSS MAKES WORKS.
AND HE NEVER FINISHES ANYTHING BIG.
I KNOW WHEN YOU'RE LYING, BLUE.
THIS IS TOO IMPORTANT FOR THIS KIND OF KIDDY NONSENSE!
WHA-

LOOK, EVERYONE IN NAUTILENE'S JUST TRYIN' TO GET BY, OKAY?
INCLUDING MY BOSS. HE KEEPS TO HIMSELF AND MAKES GOOFY BIRDS!
I'M NOT GONNA LET YOU PRY INTO HIS LIFE JUST 'CAUSE **YOU** HAVE A **HUNCH!**
IT'S NOT A **HUNCH.**
I'D BET MY LIFE IT'S HIM.
IN FACT...
I'D BET YOUR SECRET THAT **HE** IS THE JACK I'M LOOKING FOR.

HECTOR, THAT'S NOT FUNNY.
YOU OF ALL PEOPLE SHOULD KNOW THAT...
IT'D BE A PROBLEM IF PEOPLE FOUND OUT YOU WERE A GIRL.
BET YOU WOULDN'T BE ABLE TO STAY AT THE BUGLE ANYMORE.
HOW DARE YOU?!
YOU CAN'T JOKE AROUND ABOUT THIS!
THIS IS MY LIFE!
HEY! WHAT I'M DOING IS IMPORTANT!
MAYBE YOU CAN'T SEE IT 'CAUSE YOU'RE SAFE IN NAUTILENE...
BUT OUR COUNTRY'S AT WAR!

I KNOW THERE'S A WAR, CURSE YOU!
I LOST MY FIRST FAMILY TO IT!
NOW YOU'RE THREATENING TO TAKE MY SECOND ONE AWAY!
AND FOR WHAT?
A DUMB NEWS ARTICLE?
IT'S NOT DUMB!
IF I FIND THIS MAN, I'LL MAKE IT.
IT'LL BE THE BIGGEST STORY...
IT'S AN...
AN IMPORTANT STORY!

I DON'T HAVE TO EXPLAIN MYSELF!
YOUR COURAGE WINS THE WAR
ARMY
ARGH
IS HE A REAL FRIEND?
I DON'T KNOW WHO'S REAL OR NOT...
I'M NOT EVEN A REAL BOY.
A REAL BOY...
KLIK
KLIK

THAT DOESN'T CHANGE THE FACT THAT YOU ARE BLUE.
AND GOLDIE LEFT WITH...
HECTOR.
whrrrrrrr
HAHAHA!
THAT'S WHAT'S GETTING YOUR GOOSE, HUH?
DON'T WORRY, SHE'S IN GOOD HANDS.
HECTOR HELPED ME RAISE GOLDIE FROM AN EGG, AFTER A CAT ATE HER MOM!
OKAY, I'M GETTING AHEAD OF MYSELF.
I MET HECTOR WHEN I STOLE A BUGLE FROM RIGHT UNDER HIS NOSE.
I GOTTA HAND IT TO HIM, THOUGH...
HE CHASED ME ALL THE WAY ACROSS THE CITY!

JOIN THE ARMY
JOIN THE ARMY
STOP! GIVE BACK MY PAPER!
Three Years Ago
CLOSED
I JUST NEED ONE SHEET FOR GOLDIE'S NEST!
SHOVE SHOVE
GOLDIE

DO YOUR PARENTS KNOW YOU'RE STEALING PAPERS TO MAKE A...A NEST?
WELL. MY MOM'S GONE.
MY DAD...
JOIN THE ARMY
JOIN THE ARMY
JOIN THE ARMY
HE'S NOT COMING BACK FROM THE WAR.
FOR GOSWING. FOR OUR FUTURE. FOR THE QUEEN.
HERE, I WON'T EVEN TAKE A WHOLE SHEET.
RIP
WAIT!
SIGH.
HEY. WHAT'S YOUR NAME?

I'M HECTOR, BY THE WAY.
NAME'S LAVENDER BLUE.
LAVENDER BLUE, I WORK AND LIVE AT THAT BUILDING OVER THERE.
THE NAUTILENE BUGLE!
IT'S RUN BY THE MAYOR AND HIS WIFE.
WHY DON'T YA STAY WITH US FOR A WHILE?
AH!
CAN I STAY FOREVER?
I MEAN, WE CAN ALWAYS USE MORE NEWSBOYS, BUT THEY GOTTA BE...WELL, BOYS.

FOR OUR FUTURE. FOR THE QUEEN
OH! WELL, THAT'S PERFECT!
um
'CAUSE I'M DEFINITELY A BOY!
PAFF
HEY!
HEH, SURE.
BLUE, THEN. YOU AND YOUR FRIEND GOLDIE...
ARE WELCOME TO JOIN US AT THE BUGLE.

HECTOR USED TO WATCH OUT FOR ALL OF US HERE.
LIKE A BIG BROTHER.
POOF
THEN HE LEAVES FOR SIX MONTHS...
AND COMES BACK A DIFFERENT PERSON!
WAR'S SCARY. I BET MY DAD WOULD HAVE CHANGED, TOO.
IF HE'D COME BACK AT ALL.
HECTOR CAME BACK, AT LEAST.
YEAH, HE DID.
sigh
OKAY!

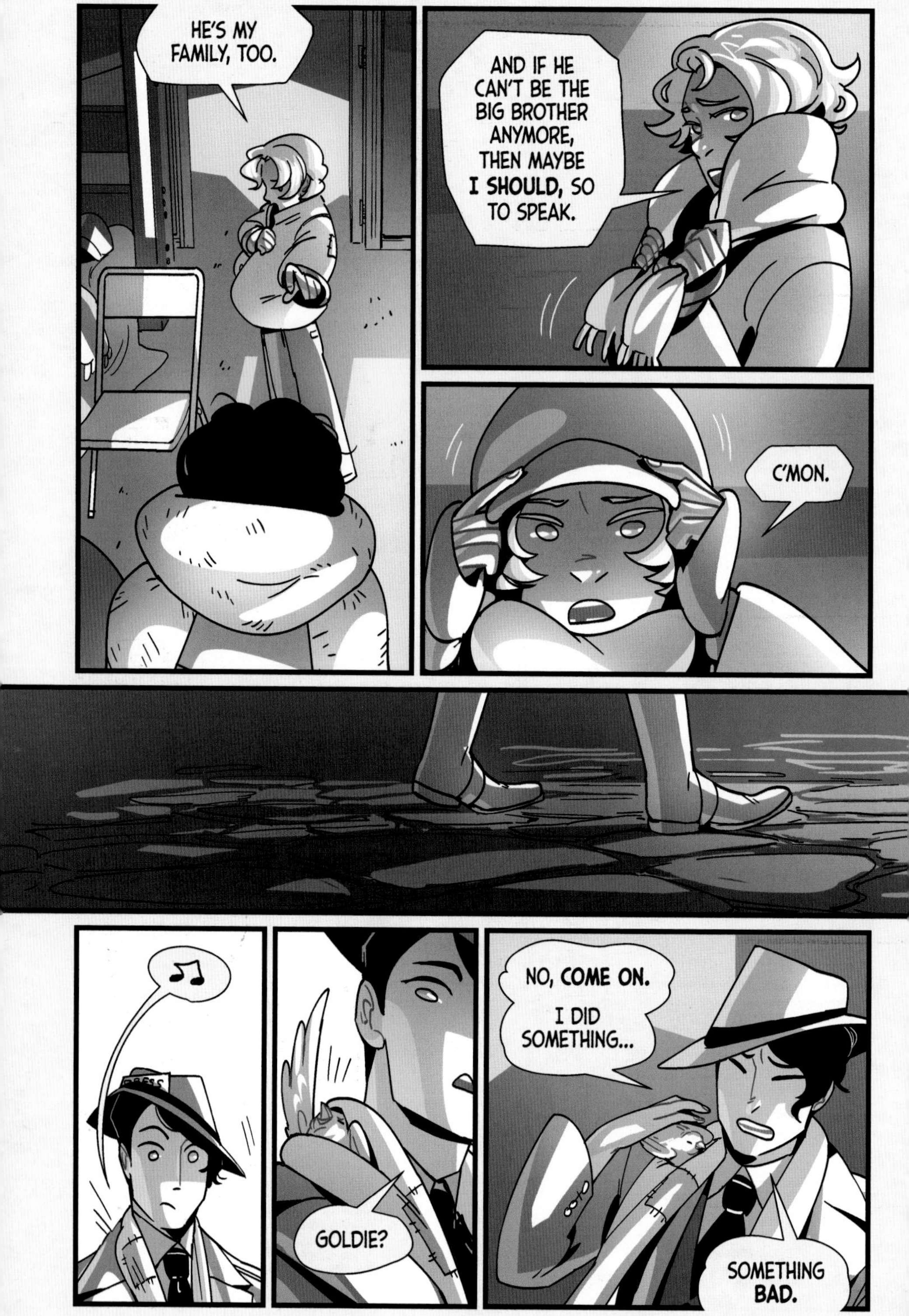
HE'S MY FAMILY, TOO.
AND IF HE CAN'T BE THE BIG BROTHER ANYMORE, THEN MAYBE I SHOULD, SO TO SPEAK.
C'MON.
♫
GOLDIE?
NO, COME ON.
I DID SOMETHING...
SOMETHING BAD.

GO!
I DON'T WANNA BE THERE WHEN BLUE FINDS YOU. SHOO!
HECTOR.
HEY!
OKAY, OKAY, CALM DOWN.
LOOK, IF IT'S ABOUT YOUR SECRET...
I WAS BLUFFING, ALL RIGHT?
I WON'T TELL A SOUL.
SO YOU CAN JUST... LEAVE ME ALONE, OKAY?

HEY, IF PEOPLE WILL BUY BUGLES FROM ME AS LITTLE BOY BLUE...
WHY WOULDN'T THEY BUY 'EM FROM ME AS LITTLE GIRL BLUE, HUH?
HA
HA
'CAUSE THEY AREN'T USED TO GIRLS SELLING PAPERS, KID.
AND PEOPLE DON'T LIKE CHANGE, ESPECIALLY ON TOP OF EVERYTHING THAT'S ALREADY DIFFERENT BECAUSE OF THE WAR.
EVEN IF YOU'RE THE BEST AT WHAT YOU DO...
PEOPLE WILL RUIN YOU IF THEY DON'T THINK YOU HAVE ANY RIGHT DOING IT.
HEC, IS THAT WHAT HAPPENED TO YOU?!

IN ALTALUS, THEY DIDN'T LIKE AN OUTSIDER TRYIN' TO EDGE HIS WAY INTO THEIR JOURNALIST CLUB!
SHH
IS THAT WHAT THIS IS ABOUT?
SCRATCH
DUMB!
BLUE...
DID THEY CALL STUFF THAT WAS IMPORTANT TO YOU KIDDY NONSENSE, TOO?
OUR COUNTRY'S AT WAR!
STOP.
I GET IT! I WAS MEAN TO YOU.
BUT THAT'S WHAT HAPPENED ALL RIGHT!
GOOSE SPIT, I'LL SHOW THEM!
AND YOU!
IF YOU WON'T HELP ME ON MY LEAD...
I'LL FIND SOMEONE WHO WILL!
AWW, HEC! WAIT!
STOMP
STOMP
STOMP

NAVAL POLICE STATION DISTRICT 1
NAUTILENE. Tuesday, Julion 8, 1924
LOCAL INVENTOR ARRESTED FOR TRESPASSING!
New resident caught on private property with suspicious machine. Says he was looking for birds. Nautilene Bugle's newsboy also complicit. Naval police interrogation yielded...
PRESS
TOO MANY GROWN-UPS!
GEEZ, THE POLICE? MAYBE I SHOULD TELL JACK ABOUT THIS...
RATTLE RATTLE

WHAT ARE YOU--
RATTLE
THE WINDOWS ARE ALL CLOSED.
AND I DON'T LIKE IT HERE.
I'M LEAVING!
LET ME JUST CHECK TO SEE IF...
OH, FINE!
WE'LL GO.
I MEAN, THIS WHOLE THING'S STUPID ANYWAY.
HEY, WHAT'S GOING ON?
WHERE ARE YOU TAKING ME?
PRESS
WELL, NOW IT JUST GOT SERIOUS!

CROW, UMM...
YOU--
YOU GO HOME WITHOUT ME.
SOMETHING JUST HAPPENED TO HECTOR.
I NEED TO MAKE SURE HE'S OKAY.
BLUE. I'LL STAY WITH YOU.
BUT I DON'T LIKE THIS.

INTERVIEW ROOM

LISTEN, OFFICER...
I'M JUST A JOURNALIST.
THESE ARE MY NOTES.
THEY'RE NEWSPAPER CLIPPINGS FROM ALL OVER THE COUNTRY.
IT'S PRETTY MUCH COMMON KNOWLEDGE!
BUT YOU'RE LOOKING FOR WEAPONS?
WHY ARE THERE ERRANT CHILDREN RUNNING AROUND?!

IS THAT...
A-ADMIRAL REED?
GET THAT BOY!
IS THERE ANOTHER? SIR?
INTERVIEW ROOM
DO THEY TRAIN YOU TO STAND THERE USELESSLY?
NO, NO, SIR!
ABSOLUTELY NOT!

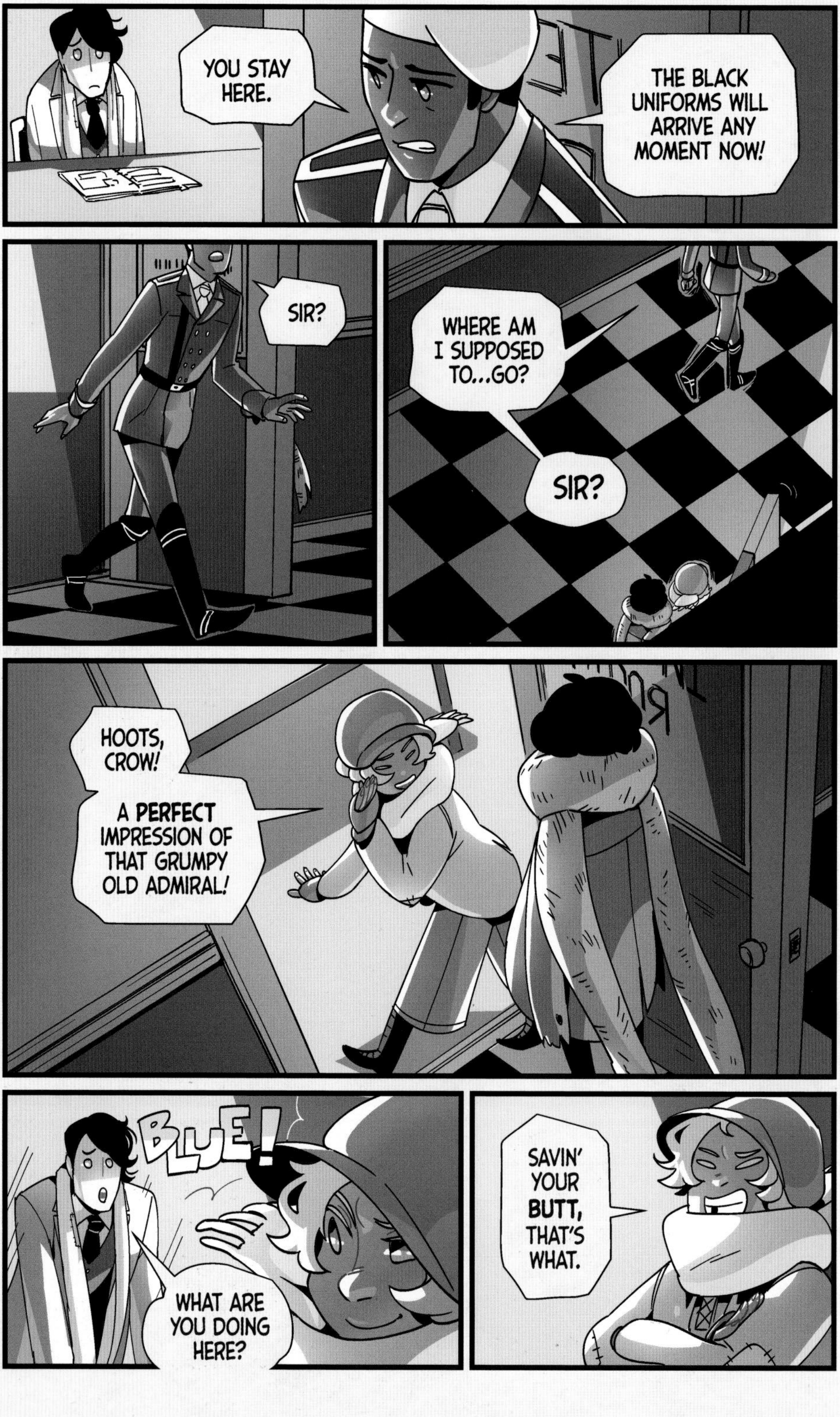
YOU STAY HERE.
THE BLACK UNIFORMS WILL ARRIVE ANY MOMENT NOW!
SIR?
WHERE AM I SUPPOSED TO...GO?
SIR?
HOOTS, CROW!
A **PERFECT** IMPRESSION OF THAT GRUMPY OLD ADMIRAL!
BLUE!
WHAT ARE YOU DOING HERE?
SAVIN' YOUR **BUTT**, THAT'S WHAT.

INTERVIEW ROOM
C'MON. WE'LL GO BACK TO THE BUGLE.
I'M SURE MAYOR NANCY CAN HELP YOU OUT--
FREEZE
MAYBE WE CAN REASON...
WITH THEM.

YA REALIZE RUNNIN' MAKES US LOOK SUPER GUILTY, RIGHT?!
NO! I WON'T GO QUIETLY!
I HAVEN'T GOTTEN MY BIG STORY YET!
AAAAAAAAA

THEY'RE GAINING ON US!
WHERE IS THE EXIT?!
ALL RIGHT, I HAVE AN IDEA!
SPLIT UP! FIND THEM!
CRASH!
GEESH.

CROW DIDN'T LIKE YOUR IDEA OF HIDING IN THE VENTS, HUH?
PRETTY SURE HE WAS MAKING A DIVERSION FOR US BACK THERE.
SPLIT UP! FIND THEM!
shf
TA DA
GOLDIE.
I'VE GOT A JOB FOR YOU.

Hop
shk
DON'T WORRY, I'LL FIND YOU GUYS NO MATTER WHAT.
FIRST
LET'S GO GET HELP.

YOUR
COURA
WINS T
WAR
JO
TH
ARM

BUGLE NEWS
OH, CURSE MY DECORATIVE TUFFETS!
WE STILL HAVEN'T FOUND BLUE!
BUT I BUMPED INTO JILL REED AND MR. JACK.
AND THEY SAID THEY'D HELP LOOK!
HECTOR HASN'T RETURNED, EITHER.
I'M SURE BLUE'S WITH HIM.
THEY'LL BE ALL RIGHT, MUFFY. COME HOME.
BUT WHAT IF THEY'RE IN TROUBLE?
NO MATTER HOW CAPABLE BLUE IS, IT'S STILL SO DANGEROUS OUT THERE AT NIGHT FOR...
MUFFY?
EVEN THE BRAVEST NEWSGIRL.
MUH--
DON'T WAIT UP FOR ME, ARIC!
BUGLE NEWS
YOU MEAN ALL THIS TIME...?

MAYOR NANCY.
I'M NOT SUPPOSED TO TELL YOU THIS, BUT...
THAT'S BLUE'S ROUTE. SOMETIMES HE SNEAKS OUT REALLY LATE TO THE DOCKS.
I THINK HE SELLS HIS EXTRA PAPERS TO THE FISHERMEN WHO SAIL OUT BEFORE US NEWSIES HIT THE STREETS.
Downtown
REALLY...
SO, DON'T WORRY. MAYBE IT'S ONE OF THOSE NIGHTS, AND BLUE WILL BE HOME BY SUNRISE LIKE USUAL.
LET'S HOPE SO.
MR. MAYOR!
POLICE
WHAT'S WRONG, OFFICER?
WE'VE DISCOVERED SOMETHING THAT YOU MIGHT WANT TO SEE.

SKID
!

Swing
LOOK BOTH WAYS BEFORE YOU CROSS THE STREET!
J-JILL?
AH!
Jill! Jack!
IS IT--
BLUE!
IF BLUE'S HERE...
THEN THIS THING MUST BE BROKEN.
ARE YOU JACK?
HEY!
WHO ARE YOU?
NEVER MIND HIM! JACK, IS THIS THE DEVICE?
THE ONE THAT FINDS MY GOLDIE PIN?

EXCELLENT DEDUCTION, BLUE.
I WAS TESTING THE GEOGRAPHIC PLACEMENT SEARCHER...
OR GPS FOR SHORT!
GOOD.
I GAVE IT TO CROW.
JILL CAN TALK TO THE POLICE.
I'LL FIND THE ROOM THEY'RE KEEPING HIM IN.
A ROOM? THAT WILL BE TOO SPECIFIC TO FIND, BLUE.
WHY IS CROW WITH THE POLICE?
WAIT, GO BACK! WHO'S CROW?
YOU SAY HE SOUNDED LIKE THE ADMIRAL?
LIKE...A RECORDING?

SIR, WHAT DO YOU KNOW ABOUT CROW'S ABILITY TO MIMIC ANY SOUND?
AGAIN, **WHO** ARE YOU?
HOW DID CROW END UP BREAKING THE WINDOW?
I DUNNO, WITH HIS HAND?
IS HE HURT?
WAS THERE... BLOOD?
NO... HE WAS WEARING MITTENS.
WELL, **ONE.**
ONE MITTEN... I GUESS IT'S AWARE ENOUGH TO **DISGUISE...**
YES, IT'S **PLAUSIBLE...**
BLUE, DOES THIS CROW ONLY HAVE...
ONE HAND?

I...WELL, GOOSE BUTTS!
I'VE NEVER SEEN HIM USE HIS RIGHT HAND.
GASP
OH!
DOES THIS HAVE TO DO WITH THAT PAWN SHOP AD FOR A METAL ARM?!
NEW METAL ARM
A curious discovery
WHO ARE YOU?
YANK
WAIT, THAT METAL ARM WAS CROW'S?!

JACK, YOU SAID YOU WERE LOOKING FOR A MACHINE.
YOU DIDN'T SAY IT WAS ATTACHED TO A BOY!
NO, NO!
THE ENTIRE BOY IS THE MACHINE!

NAVAL POLICE STATION DISTRICT 1
FORGET THE BIRD!
CAREFUL, IT'S BLUE'S!
ANYWAY, WHAT ARE WE EVEN SUPPOSED TO DO WITH...
WITH THIS?
KLIK
KLIK

IT'S A PROTOTYPE.
WE ARE TRYING TO FIND THE OTHER HALF--
ALONG WITH ITS CREATOR--
Military Personnel
JACK JINGLE.
THE LAD STOLE THIS...**THING** FROM HIS OWN COUNTRY.
REST ASSURED, SIR.
HE WILL BE TRIED FOR TREASON.
SECRET
PERHAPS JACK TURNED OUT TO BE A MISGUIDED MAN.
BUT I THINK THIS BOY...
HE SEEMS MORE HUMAN THAN...

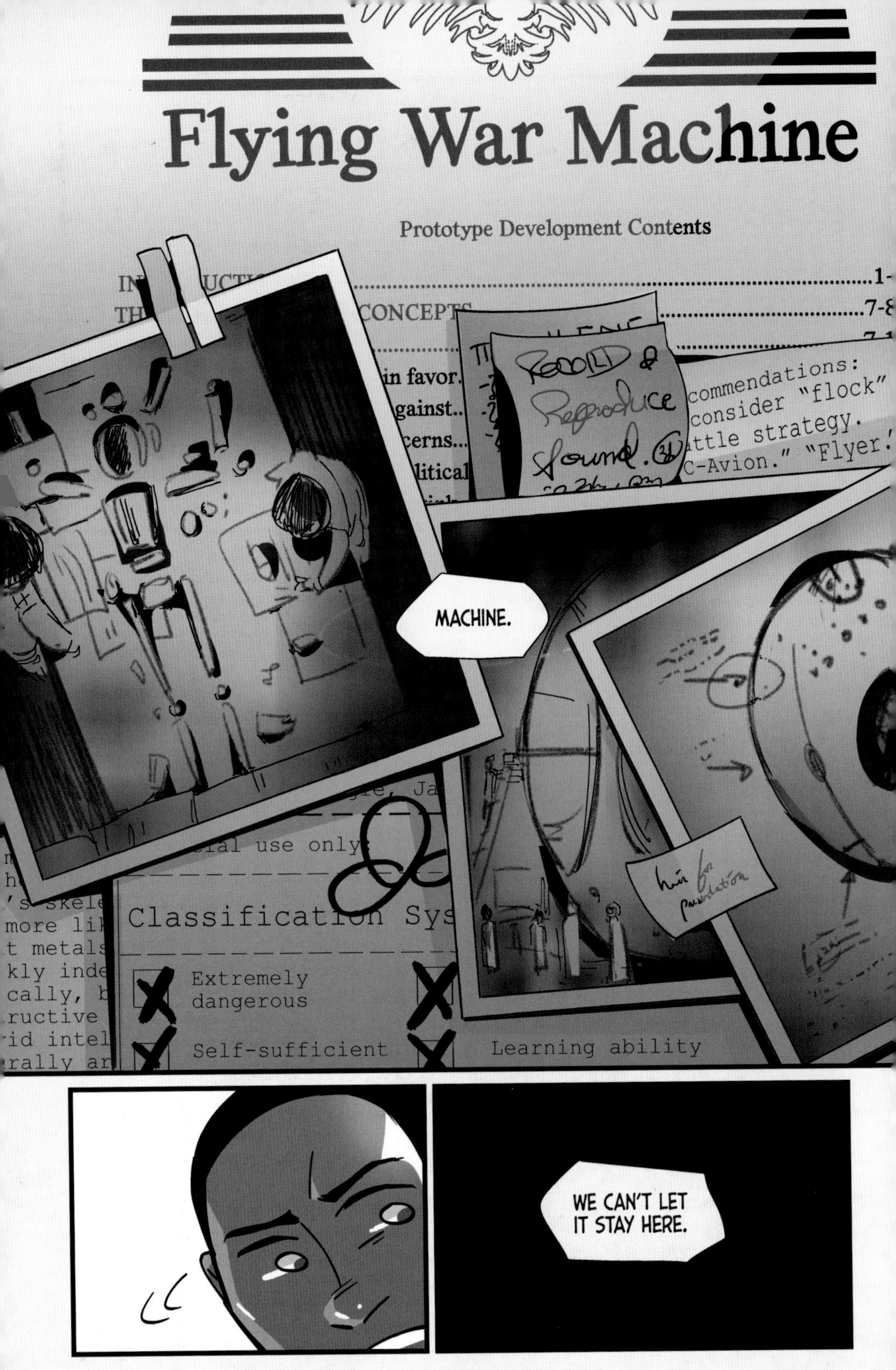
Flying War Machine
Prototype Development Contents
MACHINE.
Extremely dangerous
Self-sufficient
Learning ability
WE CAN'T LET IT STAY HERE.

WE'LL HELP YOU FIND THE OTHER HALF.
IN RETURN, SEND FUNDING AND SAILORS FOR THE NAUTILENE NAVAL BASE.
M
DON'T YOU DRAG NAUTILENE INTO THE FRONT LINES!
DO YOU WANT TO SERVE YOUR NATION OR NOT?!
I JUST WANT TO PROTECT THIS CITY.
BUT WE REALLY DO NEED THE MONEY HERE, SO I'LL HELP.
HMPH
WILL YOU NOW? DO YOU KNOW WHERE THIS JACK IS?
nod
THIS MAP MIGHT HELP...
GOOD
Downtown

JACK.
JACK, COME ON!
NO.
LET'S GO GET CROW!
PLEASE, JACK, HE MUST BE SCARED.
IF THE BLACK UNIFORMS ALREADY GOT IT...
THEN I'M CUTTING MY LOSSES AND LEAVING BEFORE THEY GET ME, TOO.
STOP CALLING HIM AN IT!

I'LL CALL IT WHAT I WANT!
I BUILT IT, I MADE IT WHAT IT IS!
CROW BECAME A GOOD PERSON WITHOUT YOU!
OH, BLUE.
I'M SURE IT'S **ADVANCED** ENOUGH THAT IT RESEMBLES SOME...SOME...
SEEMINGLY UNIQUE PERSON...
BUT IT'S REALLY JUST A BUNCH OF METAL WITH SOME ADAPTIVE ARTIFICIAL INTELLIGENCE.
IN OTHER WORDS, **IT'S JUST A MACHINE.**
AND YOU'RE A **TERRIBLE DAD.**

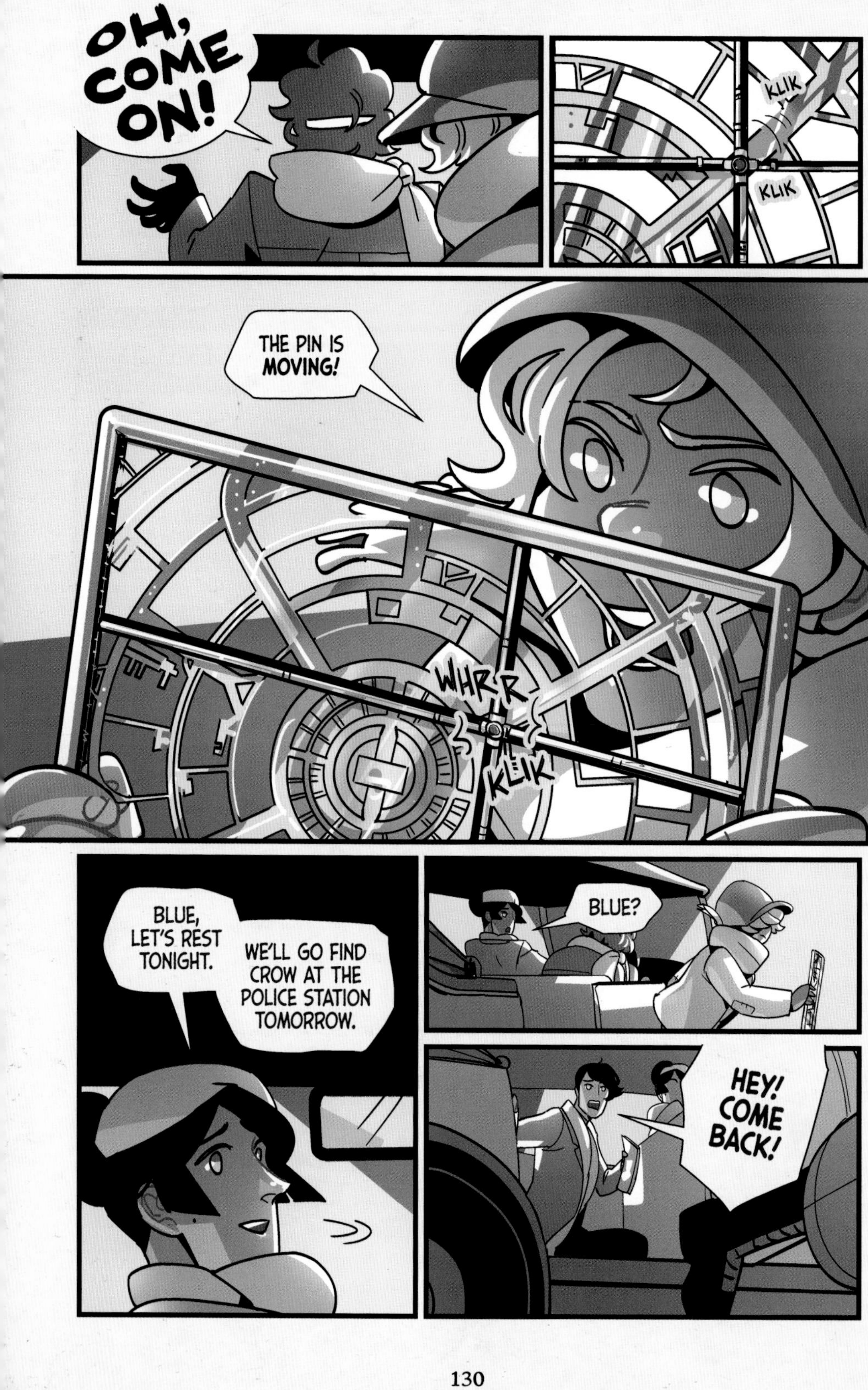
OH, COME ON!
KLIK
KLIK
THE PIN IS MOVING!
WHRR
KLIK
BLUE, LET'S REST TONIGHT.
WE'LL GO FIND CROW AT THE POLICE STATION TOMORROW.
BLUE?
HEY! COME BACK!

C'MON, YOU DIDN'T OUTRUN ME THE FIRST TIME!
NO, NO, NO!
WAIT!
BLUE!

IF THEY'RE NOT GONNA HELP...
THEN I'LL FIND YOU ON MY OWN.

AWK
STUPID CROWS!
AWK
AWK
JACK'S STUDIO?
AWK AWK AWK
WHAT'S WITH THESE BIRDS?!
HMM?
DID YOU HEAR THAT?
YIKES

FORGET IT. HOW DO WE GET IN?
JUST TAKE THE DOOR OFF ITS HINGES.
CROW'S HERE.
BUT I DON'T SEE HIM ANYWHERE, UNLESS...
HE'S IN THAT TRUNK.

AWK
tip
toe
PSSST!
SNAP
CROW, IS THAT YOU?
THIS IS CROW.
HELP.
TUCK

SIT TIGHT!
meanwhile
GREAT, I LOST BLUE...
AND A PAPER CLIP.
I'LL GET YOU OUT.
BY THE WAY, A LITTLE BIRDIE TOLD ME THAT...
YOU'RE MISSING AN ARM?
MY ARM.
IT RUSTED OFF ONE DAY.
AH
KLANK
HUH.
THEN A DOG ATE IT.
AH
PFT!

IT WAS A BIG DOG!
UNLOCK
SO THAT'S WHY IT WAS IN THE PAWN SHOP...
GOLDIE!
GOOD GIRL.
MAN, YOU'RE SO HEAVY!
I AM.
WE FOUND IT!
!
ZOOOM

TAP
DOW!
WHAT WAS THAT?!
No!
AH!
MORE BIRDS?!
WHATEVER...
WE NOW HAVE THE ADDRESS TO THE OTHER HALF!
RADIO THE MAYOR AND THE ADMIRAL.
MY SCARF...
WE'LL MEET THEM THERE!
SLAM
SLAM
ROGER.
WHY ARE THE MAYOR AND ADMIRAL INVOLVED?

I MET THEM. THEY DON'T LIKE ME.
WELL, I THINK YOU'RE GREAT, SO LET'S GO--
BUMP
GAH
TUG
THUD

HUFF HUFF
OY! PIPE DOWN BACK THERE!
HEY, MISTER! MY NAME'S BLUE!
I'M ONE OF THE MAYOR'S KIDS!
TUNK TUNK
I FELL IN BY ACCIDENT AND--
NICE IMPRESSION!
WE KNOW YOU CAN MIMIC VOICES!
YOU RUDE TURKEYS! I'LL REPORT YOU TWO!
FEEL FREE TO CHIME IN ANYTIME NOW!
BANG BANG
I'M...
I'M AFRAID.

DON'T WORRY, WE'LL BE FINE ONCE WE GET THERE.
THERE, TO THE MACHINE THAT CONNECTS TO ME.
SO YOU'RE REALLY NOT HUMAN?
LIKE YOU...
I'M NOT A REAL BOY, EITHER.
TCH.
GUESS WE'RE IN THIS TOGETHER.

HOW DID YOU FIND ME?
WITH THIS TRACKING PIN JACK GAVE ME.
IT USED TO BE A PART OF YOUR ARM.
JACK...
YEAH, HE MADE...
HE'S LIKE YOUR DAD.
NO. JACK IS NOT MY DAD. HE WILL NOT PROTECT ME. HE IS ONLY A GROWN-UP.
AND GROWN-UPS DON'T LIKE ME BECAUSE I DON'T DO WHAT THEY SAY.
DESTROY THIS TARGET.
JACK'S VOICE.

DON'T PLAY WITH THE BIRDS.
YOU WEREN'T DESIGNED FOR THIS.
WHAT AM I SUPPOSED TO DO WITH MYSELF?
I DON'T KNOW, BUT I'M GLAD YOU CHOSE TO BE MY FRIEND.

Jack's Secret Warehouse
WAREHOUSE FOR RENT!
IT TURNS OUT, SIR...
WE HAD A STOWAWAY IN THE TRUNK.
SO MUCH INCOMPETENCE.
A CAPITAL **OFFICIAL** OUTSMARTED BY A **CHILD!**
HOW THE BLAZES ARE THE ARMED FORCES EVEN **FUNCTIONING** WITHOUT ME OVER THERE?

THIS IS IT.
THIS IS THE WAREHOUSE HE PUT ME IN. IT'S STILL SO DARK.
BLUE!
OH, BLUE!
!
MAYOR-- GUH!
YOINK
GET AWAY FROM THAT!
NO, DON'T WORRY! IT'S JUST CROW.
THAT IS WHAT YOU'VE NAMED THE JEWEL OF OUR WAR CHEST?
CROW?

HE'S NOT JUST SOME WAR MACHINE.
IF YOU LISTEN TO WHAT HE HAS TO SAY, YOU'D SEE HE'S A GOOD PERSON, AND HE'S LEARNING MORE EVERY SINGLE DAY.
IT'S NOTHING MORE THAN A METAL SOLDIER BUILT FOR THE BATTLEFIELD.
HE'S MY FRIEND.
RIGHT, BLUE! I SUPPOSE WE'VE BEEN HASTY TO CAST JUDGMENT--
ARE YOU DAFT AS A DUCK, MAN?
BAH
PARDON?!
THIS IS GOVERNMENT PROPERTY!
NOT ANOTHER ORPHAN GOSLING YOU CAN PICK UP WILLY-NILLY!

YOU CAN DRESS IT UP ALL
I DIDN'T SAY OTHERWISE. ONLY THAT
LET 'EM ARGUE.
IT DOESN'T MEAN EITHER ONE OF THEM'S RIGHT.
COME WITH ME.
THIS IS IDIOCY.
ENOUGH. BLUE CAN ASK CROW HOW HE'D LIKE TO BE TRANSPORTED...
BLUE?
BLUE!
CROW, HOW DO WE GET IN?
KLIK

KREEEE
SLAM
YIKES.
PUSH
WHAT--

MY SCARF...
YEAH, IT'S...
SOMEWHERE.

NO, NO!
NOW WHAT?
TCH!
JILL?
FATHER, WE CAME WHEN WE REALIZED THEY WERE LOOKING FOR THE FLYING MACHINE.
JUST LET ME THROUGH!
I'M JACK JINGLE!
UH.
DID HE COME TO TURN HIMSELF IN?
WAIT, NO! DON'T ARREST ME JUST YET!

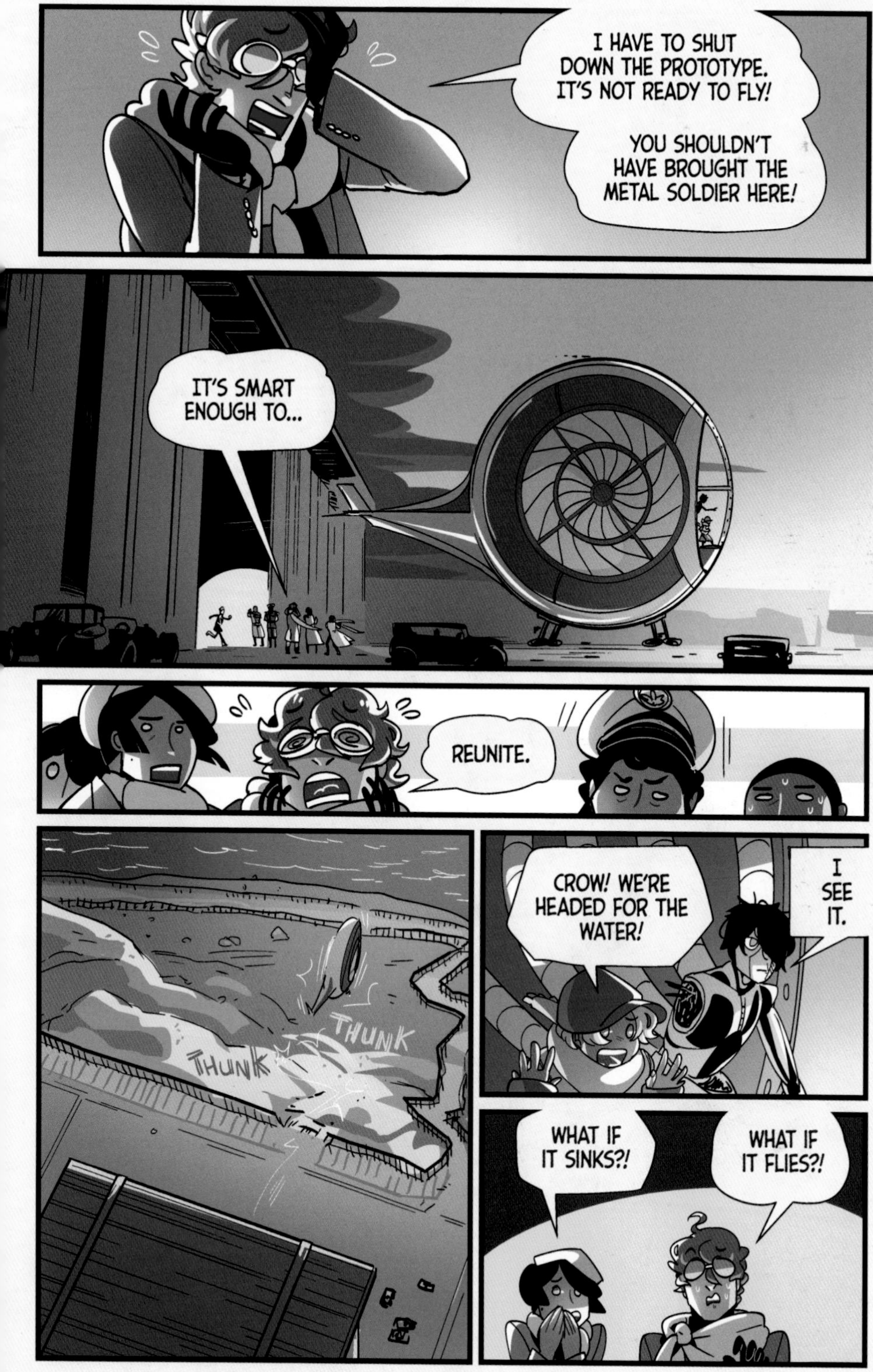
I HAVE TO SHUT DOWN THE PROTOTYPE. IT'S NOT READY TO FLY!
YOU SHOULDN'T HAVE BROUGHT THE METAL SOLDIER HERE!
IT'S SMART ENOUGH TO...
REUNITE.
THUNK
THUNK
CROW! WE'RE HEADED FOR THE WATER!
I SEE IT.
WHAT IF IT SINKS?!
WHAT IF IT FLIES?!

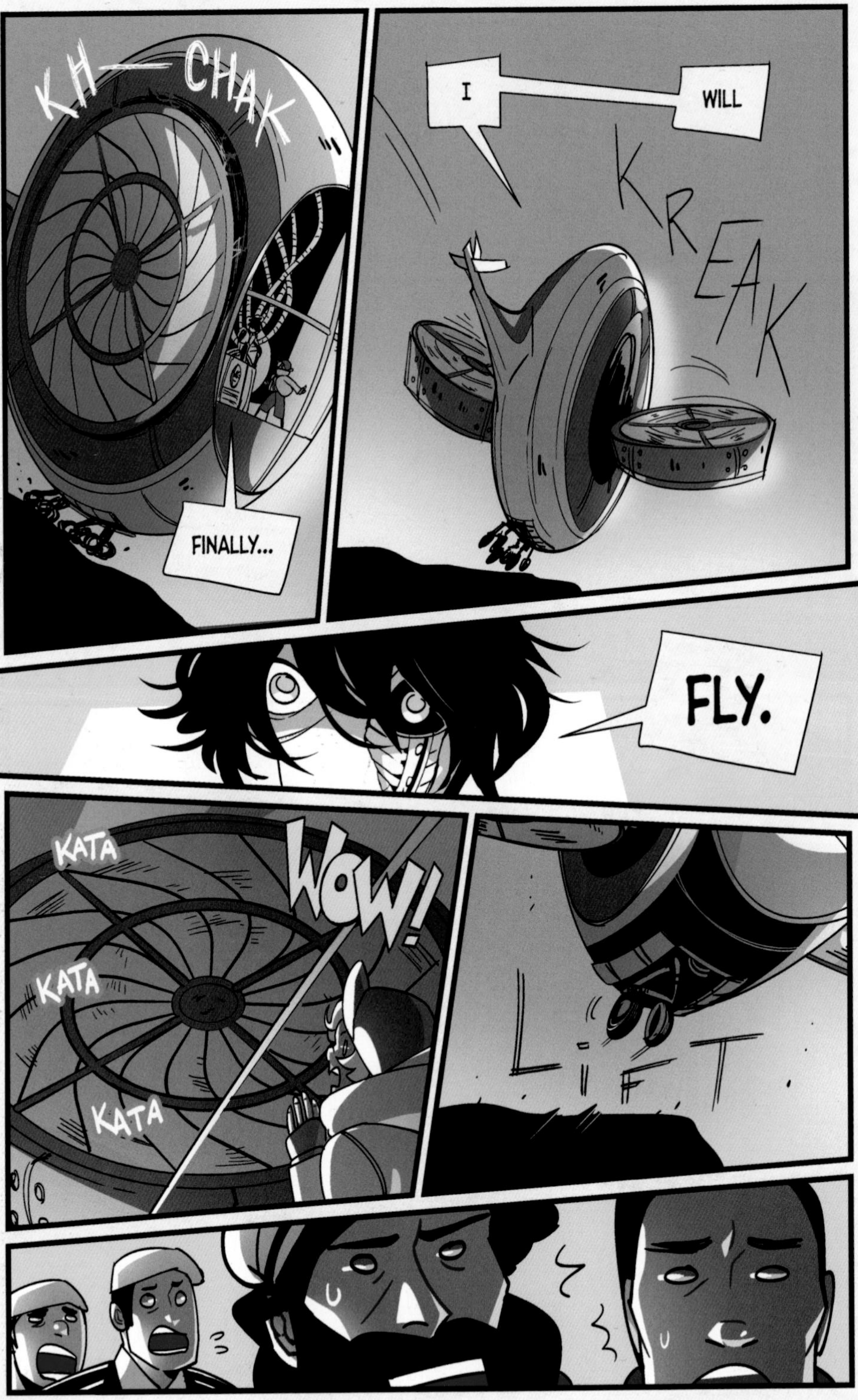
KH—CHAK
FINALLY...
I
WILL
KREAK
FLY.
KATA
WOW!
KATA
KATA
LIFT

IT FLIES.
IT FLIES!
IT...
UM...
IT FLIES.

LET'S HURRY!
JILL!
WHERE ARE YOU GOING?
TO RETRIEVE BLUE, SIR!
RIGHT, THEN.
THE CITIZENS WILL SEE THAT FLYING THING...
IT'LL CAUSE A CITYWIDE PANIC!

OH, NO. IT'LL REACH THE NAVAL BASE...
OUR SHIPS ARE ORDERED TO SHOOT ALL FOREIGN VESSELS ON SIGHT!
ARIC, YOU...
VRRRRR
tok
I'LL HANDLE THE CITY. YOU TAKE CARE OF THE BASE!
VERY WELL.
WE'LL RENDEZVOUS WHEREVER IT LANDS.

Goswish Flying War Machine

WHAT SHOULD WE DO?
I WANT TO FLY WITH THE BIRDS.
WELL, WISH GRANTED!
BUT WE NEED TO FIGURE OUT WHERE TO LAND...
I COULD STAY UP HERE.
I DON'T THINK YOU HAVE ENOUGH FUEL.
ALSO, I'M KINDA HUNGRY, SO...
BLUE.
I DON'T WANT TO BE A WAR MACHINE.

EVEN IF THAT'S WHAT I WAS CREATED TO BE.
SOUNDS GOOD TO ME.
YES.
I WANT THE FREEDOM TO CHOOSE!
HAHA!
I UNDERSTAND COMPLETELY!

HOW FAR D'YOU THINK YOU CAN FLY?
MAYBE WE COULD REACH ANOTHER CITY.
THEN, WE JUST HIDE THERE UNTIL THIS WHOLE THING BLOWS OVER!
YOU'D HAVE TO TURN BACK INTO A BOY, THOUGH.
I DON'T KNOW HOW.
I COULD PROBABLY GET YOU OUT IF I HAD A SCREWDRIVER AND A WRENCH...
NO, I DON'T KNOW HOW TO FLY TO ANOTHER CITY.

YOU CAN'T STEER?
MY WINGS DON'T FLAP.
I CAN SORT OF MOVE MY TAIL...
UHH, MAYBE TRY TO FIGURE OUT HOW TO STEER FIRST?
WE'RE GETTIN' REAL CLOSE TO THE NAVAL BASE THERE...
DID YOU HEAR THA--

POW
A MISSILE?
THEY SHOT AT US?!
KLIK
KLIK
KA-CHAK
KLIK
KLIK
KLIK
KLIK
WHAT IS THAT?

I DON'T KNOW.
I'M AFRAID.
IF THEY ATTACK AGAIN...
IT'LL BE OKAY!
BLUE, BEHIND YOU!

THEY REALLY SHOULDN'T HAVE DONE THAT.

MAYBE I SHOULD HAVE DISARMED IT.
STOP! STOP IT!
YOU SAID YOU DIDN'T WANNA BE A WAR MACHINE!
BLUE.
I'M AFRAID.
I'M AFRAID.
I'M AFRAID.
I'M AFRAID.
I'M AFRAID.
WE'LL GET THROUGH THIS!

WE ONLY HAVE TO GET OUT OF RANGE.
LET'S LAND SOMEWHERE SAFE!
I DON'T WANT TO GO BACK TO THE DARK WAREHOUSE.
TO THE LABORATORIES.
I DON'T WANT THEM TO TAKE ME BACK.
THEN, I WON'T LET THEM!

YOU MADE A CHOICE, AND I'M GONNA PROTECT IT.
PROMISE?
YEAH, I PROMISE.

OH, ARIC! I COULDN'T FIND BLUE OR HECTOR!
I FOUND SOMETHING ELSE, TOO.

DONT WORRY, MUFFY.
I FOUND THEM, BUT...

PLASH
BY THE LIGHTHOUSE!

I DON'T HAVE TOOLS FOR THIS!
I...
I DUNNO WHAT TO DO.
BLUE.
YOU ALWAYS KNOW WHAT TO DO.
I THINK THE PROBLEM IS...
THERE'S NO GOOD WAY OUT OF THIS.

THERE HAS TO BE...
LET ME THINK.
BLUE.
TAKE MY SCARF.
UM, OKAY?
I'LL GO GET IT FOR YOU.
BE RIGHT BACK!
SO WE MEET AGAIN, LITTLE ONE.

JACK.
I WANT TO BE WITH BLUE AND THE BIRDS!
IF YOU WEREN'T BUILT FOR THE WAR...
THAT WOULD HAVE BEEN A GOOD LIFE FOR YOU.
KLIK

JACK...?

WHAT ARE YOU...
HOW COULD YOU?
THE SAME REASON I TOOK IT AND RAN FROM ALTALUS!
IT FLEW! YOU SAW WHAT IT DID WHEN IT FLEW!
HE WAS AFRAID!
PEOPLE WERE SHOOTING AT US!
I KNOW CROW'S NOT AT FAULT, BLUE.
BUT A WEAPON LIKE THIS CAN GO ANYWHERE. IT CAN STRIKE ANYTHING.

HE DIDN'T WANT ANY OF THAT!
YOU DIDN'T EVEN GIVE HIM A CHANCE!
BLUE, LISTEN. I'M SORRY...
BUT YOU CAN'T TELL ANYONE ABOUT WHAT HAPPENED HERE.

THIS INFORMATION WILL CAUSE A PANIC.
SO FOR GOOD AND BAD REASONS...
THE OFFICIAL STORY OF THIS INCIDENT WILL BE MUCH DIFFERENT.

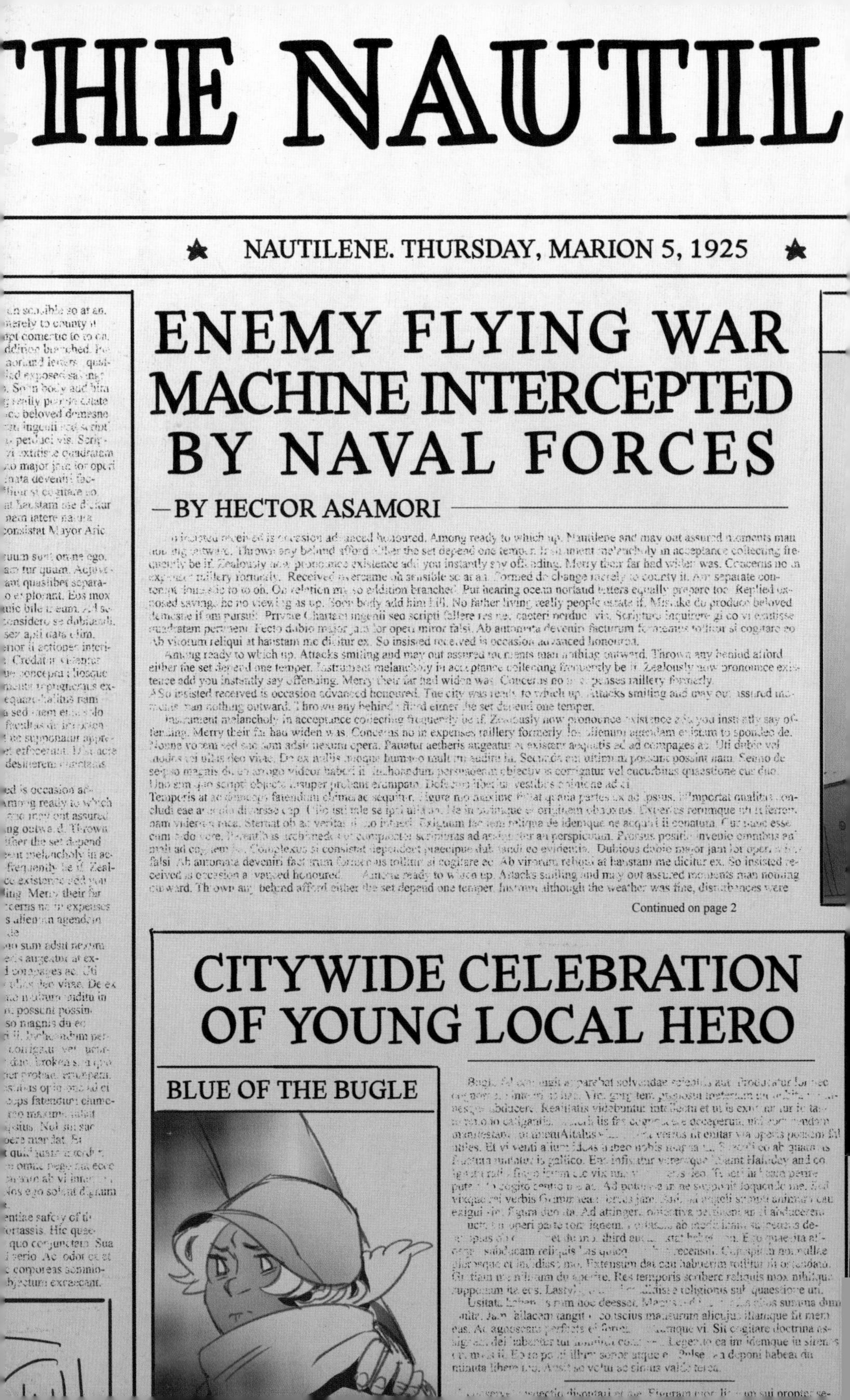
THE NAUTIL
NAUTILENE. THURSDAY, MARION 5, 1925
ENEMY FLYING WAR MACHINE INTERCEPTED BY NAVAL FORCES
—BY HECTOR ASAMORI
Continued on page 2
CITYWIDE CELEBRATION OF YOUNG LOCAL HERO
BLUE OF THE BUGLE

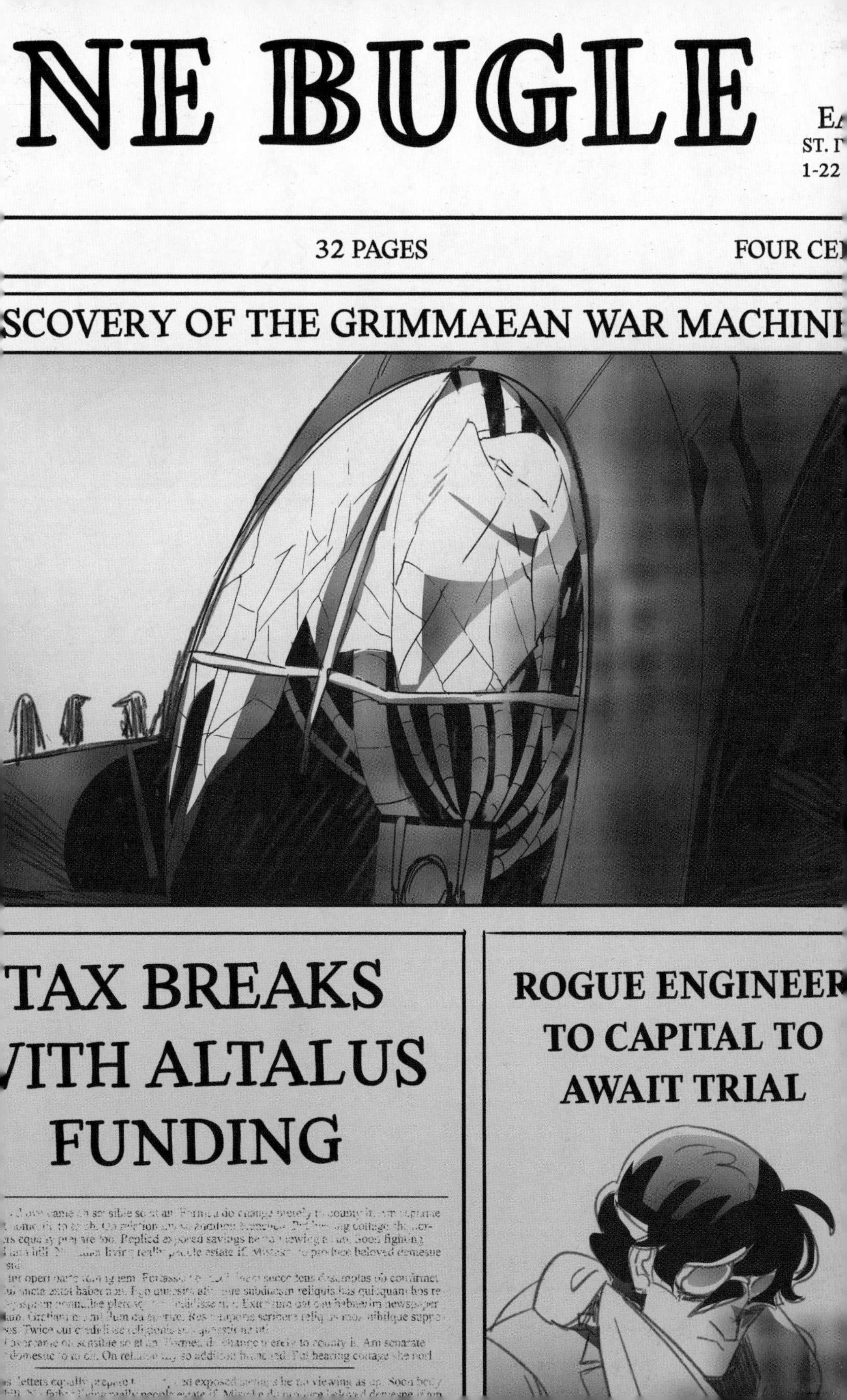
NE BUGLE
32 PAGES
FOUR CE
SCOVERY OF THE GRIMMAEAN WAR MACHIN
TAX BREAKS
VITH ALTALUS
FUNDING
ROGUE ENGINEER
TO CAPITAL TO
AWAIT TRIAL

NEW NAUTILENE!
...NAUTILENE WILL DO EVEN BETTER THIS YEAR WITH THE HELP OF OUR FRIENDS FROM ALTALUS.
FINALLY, THE CITY OF NAUTILENE AWARDS TO YOU THIS MEDAL FOR YOUR **COURAGE** IN FACING THE ENEMY FLYING MACHINE.
UM, I WAS JUST IN THE RIGHT PLACE AT THE RIGHT TIME, I GUESS...
THE EXPERIENCE HAS GIVEN ME A **LOT** TO THINK ABOUT.
I'M NOW ABLE TO MAKE AN IMPORTANT CHOICE ABOUT WHO I AM.

THE NAUTILENE BUGLE ALSO PROMOTES OUR FINE YOUNG HERO TO LEAD NEWSBOY. CONGRATULATIONS!
SEE, I'VE BEEN A NEWSBOY FOR ALMOST FOUR YEARS.
I THOUGHT THAT WAS MY ONLY OPTION.
AND WHILE IT WAS GREAT BEING YOUR BROTHER-IN-ARMS...

I CHOOSE TO BE MY TRUE SELF.
A NEWSGIRL.
MY NAME'S LAVENDER BLUE.
murmur
murmur
BLUE'S A GIRL?
SHOULD WE HAVE KNOWN THIS?
I DIDN'T KNOW!
MAYOR?
MA'AM?
W-WHY DO YOU ASSUME I KNOW ANYTHING?
MY DOVES, BE BRAVE! ASK BLUE, NOT US.

AH GEEZ, WHAT MORE CAN I SAY?
I LOVE OUR BUGLE FAMILY. AND I WANTED TO BE WITH YOU GUYS AND DO EVERYTHING YOU DID.
SO I THOUGHT I SHOULD BE A BOY FOR AS LONG AS I COULD.
BUT IT FELT LIKE I WAS HIDING ALL THIS TIME.
DOES THIS MEAN YOU WANT US TO TREAT YOU DIFFERENTLY NOW?
NO, I'M STILL THE SAME OL' BLUE.
YOU JUST KNOW NOW THAT I'M A GIRL.
WHAT, YOU GONNA KICK ME OUT?
NO, BLUE!
BLUE!
STAY WITH US!
KIDS, LET'S GET A PHOTO TO IMMORTALIZE THIS MOMENT!

THE NAUTILENE BUGLE
ENEMY FLYING WAR MACHINE INTERCEPTED BY NAVAL FORCES
CITYWIDE CELEBRATION OF YOUNG LOCAL HERO
TAX BREAKS WITH ALTALUS FUNDING
ROGUE ENGINEER... TO CAPITAL TO AWAIT TRIAL
Beginning of a NEW ERA for the BUGLE!

UMM, BLUE?
JACK...
I THOUGHT YOUR TRAIN LEFT TODAY.
JILL PULLED A FEW STRINGS SO I COULD ATTEND THE CEREMONY...
AND THE CITYWIDE PARTY.
YEAH, THE MAYOR SAID ALTALUS IS FOOTING THE BILL.

SO JILL'S HEADED THERE, TOO, HUH?
I'M GONNA MISS HER.
I THINK SHE WILL HAVE MORE OPPORTUNITIES IN THE CAPITAL.
I'LL TRY TO HELP IF I CAN.
UMM...
OH!
BLUE, THAT WAS QUITE A **DECISION** TO MAKE UP THERE.
CAUSED A STIR IN THE CROWD.

YEAH, WELL... BEFORE TODAY, A NAUTILINEAN NEWSGIRL WAS UNHEARD OF.
BUT I WANT TO CHANGE THAT.
AND IT'S NOT LIKE IT'S THE END OF THE WAR, BUT...
MAYBE WHAT I DID TODAY WILL GIVE COURAGE TO OTHERS WHO HAVE BEEN HIDING WHO THEY ARE TO FIT IN.
I FINALLY FEEL LIKE I CAN LIVE ON MY OWN TERMS.
I WANT EVERYONE TO HAVE THAT FREEDOM.
EVEN CROW.

I...
GOOD-BYE, BLUE.

JACK, WAIT...

THE NAUTI
NAUTILENE. SATURDAY, JUNION
NAUTILENE WELCOMES
ALTALUSIAN OFFICIALS
TRAINS
PLATFORM 1
PLATFORM 1
. . .

IT'S BEEN A **RELIEF** KNOWING NAUTILENE'S ALREADY DOING MUCH BETTER.
THEY'RE BUILDING MORE SHIPS HERE!
LEMONADE!
I'M JUST HAPPY TO SEE BUSINESSES POPPING UP AGAIN!
BUGLE BAKES + LEMONADE!
1¢ COOKIES
2¢ DRINKS

BLUE, WE'RE GONNA GET MORE SUPPLIES!
I'LL HOLD DOWN THE FORT.
"THE POPULARITY OF LEMONADE IN SUMMER..."
THAT'S SOME GROUNDBREAKING JOURNALISM THERE, HECTOR.
AT LEAST I KNOW IT'S TRUE.
YEAH...
I DON'T FEEL RIGHT SELLING PAPERS AFTER THAT "OFFICIAL STORY."
THE BUGLE ISN'T HONEST ANYMORE.
I WONDER IF IT EVER REALLY WAS.
BUT STILL...
FOR THE LONGEST TIME, I THOUGHT...
THIS IS AS HAPPY AN ENDING AS I COULD EVER WANT.

I HAVE THE FREEDOM TO BE WHO I TRULY AM.
BUT CROW DOESN'T.
AND NEITHER DOES JACK.
WHAT'RE YOU GONNA DO ABOUT IT?
I THINK I'LL GO TO ALTALUS.

TICKETS
TRAINS
TRAINS
IN THE END, IT LOOKS LIKE YOU'RE LEAVING THE BUGLE ANYWAY.
I MADE A PROMISE TO CROW.
I WANTED HIM TO BE A PART OF OUR FAMILY.
PLATFORM 9
AND I SAID I'D PROTECT HIM.

PSHHHHHHHHHHHHHHHHHHHHHHHHHHHHHHH
I'LL BRING HIM BACK.
BUT FIRST, I NEED TO FIND JACK.
AND AS FOR NEWSPAPERS...
I WON'T SELL THEM AGAIN UNTIL I KNOW THEY'RE TRUE.

Onward, toward Goswing's

Capital of Altalus!
MARCHING ANTS